Inheritance

by

Angela Bradley

Published by New Generation Publishing in 2017

Copyright © Angela Bradley 2017

First Edition

The author asserts the moral right under the Copyright, Designs and Patents Act 1988 to be identified as the author of this work.

All Rights reserved. No part of this publication may be reproduced, stored in a retrieval system or transmitted, in any form or by any means without the prior consent of the author, nor be otherwise circulated in any form of binding or cover other than that in which it is published and without a similar condition being imposed on the subsequent purchaser.

www.newgeneration-publishing.com

New Generation Publishing

Prologue

Autumn 2015

It was the flash of white amongst the dark soil that alerted the JCB driver, forcing him to climb down from his cab to take a closer look. He had been digging a trench from the old stable block at Oakdene Manor across a stretch of lawn to the road. The owners of the Manor were changing the old buildings into holiday cottages so needed water and other facilities to be provided. It was often difficult disturbing ground that hadn't been touched for a long time because no-one knew what lay beneath the surface. He'd found all sorts during his working life, ants nests, boulders, unknown water pipes, even buried treasure.

"What is it this time?" muttered Phil as he looked down into the newly excavated hole.

His face suddenly turned grey and he erupted in a cold sweat. Turning he raced towards the buildings shouting, "Carl! Carl! --- Quick! --- Come here ---."

He darted round the corner into the arms of his fellow workmen who'd heard his yells. They tried to calm him down but Phil, overweight and asphyxiated with horror was a shuddering mass of palpitating flesh.

"There's a sk-sk-ull." He pointed towards the way he had come, " ---with teeth --- clothes, a bit of hair. -- It's horrible."

Carl, the foreman, telling everyone to stay put, rushed around to see what he feared would put a stop to their construction work, whilst the others sat Phil down and gave him some water, trying to calm him.

However curiosity got the better of them and leaving their terrified mate to recover, followed the boss round to the other side of the stables where he was leaning over the newly dug trench.

There was silence, a silence born of disbelief. They saw

what Phil had seen, a skull with some straggly bits of hair attached, and a skeleton, partly covered with soiled material.

"Oh, my God," one man said. "Is it a man or a woman?"

"The clothing looks like a dress -- or a blouse."

"A woman," said another, " I wonder who she was, --- and how long she's been there."

"Was she --uh -- murdered, do you think? " said a third man. "You don't just bury someone like that," and the gang of normally tough builders moved back from the scene of the crime, feeling shocked, horrified and definitely shaky.

"I'll phone the Police," said Carl. "We'll have to stay here until they come and then they'll cordon the whole place off. There'll be no more work done on this site, until they've investigated. I'll have to get onto the owners, the Sheppards. They'll be shocked at the discovery. They've not lived here long but, as Mrs. Sheppard inherited this house from the previous owners, she'll have to be questioned."

Part 1

Chapter One

A few months earlier

This was a moment to treasure. One they had feared they would never see. The newly decorated entrance hall sparkled in fresh colours and the sun mottled the oak floor with a latticed pattern, as Anna stood, silhouetted in this elegant setting with her eyes on James as he stretched to hang the recovered painting above the stone fireplace.

"Will that do?" he asked, stepping back to see how the picture looked.

"Wonderful," said Anna, smiling and clapping her hands, whilst behind her the shadows moved as if her parents were nodding their heads in approval.

"The first of many I hope," said James, hugging his wife, as they looked at the superb Cotswold scene painted in oils by the famous artist, John Dunstable, that Anna's father, William, had bought as part of his collection. The painting was of their house, Oakdene Manor, in its prominent position next to the church in the small village of Westford.

"So what do we do with this one?" asked Anna as she bent to pick up the discarded painting that the other had replaced and which, to most people's eyes looked exactly the same.

"Wrap it up and store it," said James. " Who knows when we might need it, " he laughed. "It is, actually, a very good copy." And so it was. It had fooled a great many people, themselves included, hanging as it had, for many years in exactly the same spot as the original.

Anna sat on the old settle by the fire and watched James as he swathed the unwanted painting in bubble wrap and brown paper.

"I'll put it in the attic," he said, and hurried off.

It had been such a big decision to give up jobs, friends, their own house, to come and live in this imposing Cotswold manor. They had known that the day would come when Anna would inherit the property from her mum and dad, Celia and William, but had shrugged off the prospect until the dreaded day occurred.

But when it did their world had been turned upside down. Anna's inheritance was not the prosperous estate and beautiful house that she had expected but a ransacked property bereft of anything of value and a fortune that had completely disappeared. They moved in realising the struggle they would have, to finance their needs and keep the house and estate from being sold, but also determined to try to retrieve some of the money that had been so deviously stolen from them.

Oakdene Manor hadn't always been her home. She'd grown up in Bristol, had moved many times into larger, more spacious houses. Her father William was one of the worlds' great optimists, an opportunist who lived by his wits and ability to speculate.

She remembered his enthusiasm when, as a child, she listened as he told her about his early life helping his father on the market stall selling fruit and vegetables. He'd loved the whole experience, learned how to shout loudly and entice people with his knowing grin, to buy more than they really wanted. He had realised very early that the road to prosperity was to acquire money and lots of it. He knew that his own dad would never be rich because he spent what he earned the moment he got it, drinking, betting and enjoying himself.

"You take life too seriously Billy, lad," he would say but William, seeing his mum struggling to make ends meet and bring up three children had no desire to echo her life of hardship.

Anna wandered into the lounge and sat in the window seat looking out. She could hear James mowing the grass.

She thought again of her dad's moneymaking stories

when he was a boy, how he sold his sweets rather than eating them himself, loaned his bike for payment, ran errands for neighbours especially the older ones and all the time saving up the rewards that came his way. He was never at home. He proudly told Anna about the many times people praised him, to his mother.

"Your lad's got a heart of gold, Mrs."

His canny moneymaking activities didn't stop, even when studying at school.

He won a place at the local Grammar school, found Maths fascinating. University wasn't for him. He hadn't the time nor his parents the money, so smartening himself up went for a job in a local bank. The world of finance at his feet he climbed the ladder, spent his savings on shares wisely and decided that, land, property and housing was what the country needed.

It was the late 1950's and more land was being bought for houses to satisfy the growing post war population.

"So I bought some and started to build," her dad had said, proudly.

There had been no stopping him. With a nose for a bargain his empire had grown.

By the 1980's he had offices and estate agencies all over the West country and it was whilst visiting his Cheltenham branch one day that he read a letter from Sir Roland Williams requesting an appointment concerning the sale of his house Oakdene Manor and the estate lands that went with it.

He'd immediately spotted a sale of considerable value and decided to visit the gentleman himself. It turned out to be a momentous decision and one that would change his life completely.

Anna moved towards the piano. She often played. She had inherited the talent from her mother. This piano, a Bechstein Grand had been bought for her mum by her dad as a present when they first moved into Oakdene Manor and had the space to house it.

On the piano many photos stood, of her parents and herself, other relatives and friends but sadly no brothers and sisters. Her mum's series of miscarriages had left Anna an only child.

She looked at a picture of her mother and then of her parents wedding. Her dad had always said that he was very lucky that she chose him for a husband, but attraction works both ways. She may have been the daughter of a well-to-do farmer with a private school education but one look at the admiring grin of young William, bank clerk as he was then, had been enough for her mum to realise that no other man in the world would do. It wasn't long before her family had discovered that her sudden desire to draw the workers' wages from the Bank each week was so that she could see and speak with the personable young man behind the counter.

Her mother had looked dazzling in her wedding dress and kept it carefully packed in a box. It wasn't here now. Anna had looked but it was something else that had disappeared and been added to the list of missing items.

Her mum's family had not expected the marriage to last. They deemed her father's background to be considerably inferior to their own.

"My dad nearly drunk the bar dry at the reception," her dad had told her, "but my mum bundled him into a cab and took him home early, not wanting him to cause a scene."

"Your mum was very happy to be a humble housewife and I to mix with the agricultural community," her dad had said. "A good suit, money for drinks and a farmer's daughter for a wife stood me in good stead in farming circles."

Anna looked around at the room now furnished mostly with her own furniture. Everything of value that her mother had bought and acquired had gone, and she felt sad when she looked at the place where the grandfather clock had been that she had helped her father to choose and the chaise longue that she had bought to replace the pretty love seat that was also no longer there.

"I treated the old couple with respect," her father had said. "They were finding the house and estate too expensive and too large. They had no heirs, both sons had predeceased them. The heart had gone out of their world. They only had each other and wanted to leave the house that held so many memories and move to somewhere smaller and more comfortable, so I helped them. I gave them a reasonable price for a quick sale and used my agency in Weston-Super-Mare to find them an apartment by the sea. So we were all satisfied. I was the proudest man in the world when we drove through the gates and up the drive and saw your mother's face as she looked at her new home.

"Not bad for a barrow boy, eh Anna?" her father had said, proudly.

Anna walked up the wide oak staircase, her hand touching the beautiful finish of the shining banister. She moved along the corridor to her old bedroom. She'd chosen it as it overlooked the sloping garden that stretched to the shallow stream where water rats lived and tiny minnows swam.

It hadn't changed much, just looked unused, impersonal. She'd been fifteen when they'd moved and was a boarder at a private school in Clevedon. She'd spent her first holiday making the room comfortable. Her father had indulged her with sound systems and TV. She had built in wardrobes, a large bed and colourful fabrics. The floor had been covered in a soft carpet and all her precious possessions, books, records etc. had filled the shelves along one wall. It was large as bedrooms go and she had been the envy of her school friends, when they came to stay. They had all slept in her room as she had a bed settee and a mattress that pushed under the bed when it wasn't needed.

Anna could still see the outlines of posters that had filled the walls but the room didn't seem hers any more. Her mother's nurse, Helen, had used the room during her period of stay there.

She looked in the mirror, still the one that had reflected her image so long ago. Now the face of a forty-five year old peered back at her. She was very like her mother, bouncy hair flecked with grey, eyes that could look severe to her pupils, and a smile that had won James' heart.

Her present bedroom that looked out onto the sweeping drive lined with oak trees never seemed to be hers. She and James had moved into it as it was the master bedroom with an en suite bathroom but she saw her parents in every shadow, even though she had bought new furniture, sold her mum's bed and refurbished it. The sorrow that she had felt when she had entered the room after her mother's death and seen the few possessions that had been left behind had never left her.

The wardrobe that had once been filled with beautiful clothes, the jewellery boxes full of valuable necklaces and rings, and drawers containing a medley of scarves, gloves and fine lingerie had been rifled through and little of value left.

Across the corridor was her son, Adam's room, not one to be entered without taking a deep breath first. All chaos ruled inside when he was at home, but at the moment he was at Bristol university and Anna had cultivated some order, before the next time he came home and repeated his determination to scatter all his clothes on the floor and strew the furniture with dirty plates and mugs with their lingering, suspicious smells. The problem was that he was an idealist, hadn't time for everyday humdrum. His head was full of solutions, anything that would improve the natural world. He would march with protestors against anything that would spoil the environment especially where agricultural land had been bought for other purposes including housing. Anna could imagine the arguments he would have had with his grandfather about it, but as he was only five when he died they were all saved the drama of them.

She moved downstairs and along the passage to the back of the house. *This place really is too big for us, she thought,* as she walked into the warmth of the old kitchen. It needed modernising but she couldn't bear to change it. The aga still functioned marvellously. She'd spent many hours, at home in the holidays, sitting in the old comfy chair with her feet on its warmth, reading. Occasionally Hazel, their cleaner, from the village had come in and laughed at her,

"You'll get chilblains, m'dear and your feet'll itch." but Anna's reply was,

"It's so warm and cosy sitting here." Hazel, however had been well aware that the kitchen's other visitors Tom and Ben, the gardeners, were the main attraction when they came in for their tea. Ben, young, tall and full of fun teasingly always brought blushes to Anna's teenage cheeks.

Now there was just herself, James and occasionally Adam. James had wanted her to have some help in the house but she disliked the idea of strangers poking about. Hazel had developed arthritis and given up work and her daughter Jenny was employed in the office of a department store in Cheltenham. Helen had also gone after her mum had been admitted into a home. What had happened to her mother and her possessions still lingered in her mind and anyway Anna wanted to be busy. She'd been a teacher, for goodness sake, where days never seemed to be long enough and this life change and less pressure took some getting used to.

Time to get some tea and call James she thought. He lived and breathed the estate, night and day, just as if he'd been born to it. After tea they would search the web trying to locate auction sites, sales, e bay offers, anywhere for signs of some of the paintings and precious items that had been taken from the house during her mum's illness. Anna and James had previously compiled a list when Elliott first came on the scene, of valuables in the house and information about the original paintings and some photos of precious items, silver, jewellery etc. This list had been lodged with the estate's solicitor for insurance purposes. Thankfully Evan Pugh had been stalwart in his refusal to part with them to Elliot when he asked, saying that Anna was the only person allowed to view them.

She prepared a lasagne and some salad then went to the back door to look for James. She could see him cleaning the mower in the outhouse.

"Tea's ready," she called.

"Coming," he answered.

Anna stood, watching him and recalled another memory, one that she would never forget. It was the summer of 2000. She and Adam had come to stay for a week during the holidays.

"Call your father," her mum had said and Anna had gone to the study, opened the door and called, "Tea's ready, dad."

She had found him, sitting at his desk, but he had not answered her because, to her horror, she had seen that his head was tilted back and his eyes were wide open.

She had rushed to him but realised that there was nothing she could do. There wasn't a breath of life in him.

Chapter 2

James crossed the yard and went into the kitchen. He was a tall, good-looking man with a mop of greying hair. He'd led a hectic working life as a doctor eventually becoming a consultant in a hospital. Idleness was not on his agenda and taking over the estate duties was a challenge that he relished. He kicked off his shoes, put on some slippers and went to the sink to wash his hands, then sat down with a sigh at the large, wooden table. They always ate in the kitchen when they were on their own, so it didn't matter that he was in his working clothes.

"Well, that's a good job done," he said. "I've built up an appetite. What's for tea?"

" Lasagne," said Anna. She sounded a bit down.

"You OK?" he asked.

"I've just been remembering dad and the day he died. It's almost fifteen years ago."

"He wouldn't have liked what's happened to his hard earned fortune," said James.

"I still feel so guilty that I didn't know what was going on," said Anna. "I was too busy climbing the success ladder."

"He would have appreciated that."

"--- and then, five years ago there was mum, in a home, and I had to -- wanted to visit her as often as I could."

"No more recriminations, now. It's all in the past. We're over the worst, still solvent and the old house is looking good again. "

They finished their meal.

"Go into the lounge. I'll bring in the coffee," said James.

Anna's thoughts were still with her parents. Fifteen years seemed a long time since her dad's death. He'd had a sudden heart attack. There was nothing anybody could have done. The horror of the moment when she had found him would remain with her forever, but surprisingly her mother's resilience had been amazing. In the depths of the night Anna had heard her sobbing which had stimulated her own misery but daily, amongst people, she had put on a brave face, accepted their sympathy and had become determined to carry on running the estate in her dad's memory.

She thought about his funeral. It had been a stately occasion attended by tenants, employees, business acquaintances and villagers. The church had bulged at the seams and many unlucky mourners had been forced to stand outside. Her dad had been buried in the churchyard, and a large area had become covered with wreaths and flowers. All the mourners had been invited back to the Manor as if in respect to their feudal lord and refreshments set out on the lawn in view of the river, woodland and the landscape that her dad had grown to love.

They had later withdrawn to the lounge as Anna had seen that her mum looked tired. It had been an exhausting day.

"Why don't you go and have a lie down, mum?" she'd suggested. "You look all in."

"I won't sleep tonight, if I do," she'd said. "In any case it's nice to have the house full. I'll just go and see if Harriet wants a cup of tea."

Her dad's older sister, Harriet had been staying for a few days. The two had become very close after their mother had died and her dad had helped her financially since she'd become a widow.

Anna thought about her aunt. She had taken her brother's death very hard. They'd had a tough childhood, their dad eventually dying from too much drink and their mother, who'd struggled all her life had found herself alone and with little money. Anna's dad had bought her a small, modern house, not far from her friends, making visiting easy.

Her aunt had never had children and her mum had

known that the loss of her brother, William, was as upsetting and desperate for his sister as it was for herself.

When her mum had left the room Anna recalled her conversation with James, "Perhaps Aunt Harriet could be persuaded to come and live with mum. They've always got on well together and this is such a big house."

"It would be more sensible if your mother sold it," James had said. "She could buy something smaller and more suitable. They could still live together, go on foreign holidays, cruises. Your mum would have plenty of money."

"You know what she'd say if you suggested it," Anna had said, cynically. "This house was dad's dream, the culmination of his success. I'm sure she'll never sell."

"But it's far too big for her. It was enormous when there were two of them."

"She'll have Hazel to clean. Someone to pop in every day."

"But it's not enough is it?"

"Then there's the estate to run, farms to oversee, rents to collect."

"But your dad hired an estate manager to do all that. David will carry on, I'm sure, and won't want her interfering."

By that time her mum and aunt Harriet had come in with the tea and set it down on a low table.

"Should our ears be burning?" her mum had asked.

"We were just wondering how you're going to feel about living here by yourself," said James. "This house is lovely when it's full but just think what it will be like when we've all gone, ------ quiet, large and expensive to run."

"What if Aunt Harriet came to live here permanently," Anna had suggested. You two get on so well together."

"We've talked about that," Aunt Harriet had said, "and the idea of it is lovely. Celia knows that I love coming to visit and will come more often, but I'm settled in Bristol, have lots of friends, am involved with the church. I'd miss my Bingo, Mother's Union and Whist drives. I'm too old to start all over again. Please don't make me feel that I'm being selfish," and the tears that were easy to shed on this doleful day, had tumbled down Harriet's cheeks.

Anna had hurried over with some tissues.

"Auntie, I'm sorry. We were only thinking of ways to help mum. James and I feel the same. Moving here at this time would be difficult for us - not impossible, but we're both working our way up the job ladders. I'm in the running for deputy head and James hoping for a consultancy at the hospital. Adam also has just settled at school. Dad's sudden death has set all our lives in turmoil."

The solemn atmosphere had been suddenly interrupted by a call from the kitchen.

"We're home." Hazel's daughter, Jenny had called, returning with Adam. They'd been out for the day. Jenny had kindly offered to look after Adam who was great friends with her own children, Nell and Matthew. A funeral was no place for a five year old who didn't really understand death and the results of it. He did know that he wouldn't see his grandad again and this had caused Anna to hug him tightly and let her emotions flow with his.

She smiled when she remembered Adam charging in with his usual exuberance and flinging himself on James.

"Did you enjoy the swimming baths?" Anna had asked.

"I swam across from one side to the other, and I only put my feet down once."

"Well that's wonderful."

"Can we go again soon?" he'd asked.

"I'll take you," said James, "before I go back at the weekend."

"Can Nell and Matthew come too?"

"Of course."

"How was the rest of the day," Anna had asked Jenny.

"We gorged ourselves in Pizza Hut, then went to the park---"

" --and we went in a row boat on the lake," Adam had said. "Jenny rowed. She was rubbish. We nearly fell in."

"Shush," Jenny had said, laughing. "You weren't

supposed to tell them that!"

Anna had asked Jenny if she wanted some tea or a cold drink.

"No I'm fine, thanks. When we got back we lit the barbecue and cooked hot dogs."

"They were yummy," said Adam.

Jenny had then asked, "How did things go here? I'm sorry I wasn't with you."

"Don't be. You helped us no end. In a way it was a wonderful send off for dad. So many people came. He had a lot of friends, was greatly respected and the weather for once made it perfect for being outdoors. The old house would have been bursting at the seams if they'd all had to come inside."

Jenny had then left saying wearily, "I'd better go and get my two to bed."

Anna had thanked her, and Adam, in his usual robust way, had thrown himself on her giving her a big hug. "Thanks Jenny - love you."

Tears had glistened in her eyes as she'd hugged the little boy who had just lost his grandad, and she hurried from the room.

Adam had then started to roll about on the floor with the two dogs. There had always been dogs at Oakdene Manor. At the moment there were two very dissimilar ones, a grey graceful whippet called Mitzy and a small Cavalier King Charles spaniel, whose name was Bonnie. They had both been acquired rather than sought after, Mitzy from a new born litter given to William by one of his tenants and Bonnie from a friend who had moved abroad.

They had been William's exercise companions, walked the estate with him every day, joined by Adam when he came to stay and was considered old enough to go for long treks with his Grandad.

Anna had looked at him stroking Bonnie, happy after a day out knowing that he would feel the loneliness of not having his grandad to walk with any more. A great empty gap had appeared in their lives and she recalled her sadness at knowing how hard this gap would be to fill.

She had left Aunt Harriet and her mum dozing, shattered after a traumatic day and taken Adam off to bed. He'd said goodnight to James and plodded up the stairs. His busy day had made him very tired. Anna knew that he would fall fast asleep as soon as his head hit the pillow.

"I'll take the dogs out," James had said. "They've been cooped up all day. Mitzy, Bonnie," he'd called and the two eager dogs had joyfully rushed after him.

Anna suddenly brought herself back to the present as James came in with the coffee.

"You seem to be miles away."

"I was just remembering dad's funeral. It was wonderful how so many people turned out to pay their respects."

"All except one, of course."

"Aunt Gwenda."

Immediately their mood changed.

"That woman," growled James. "I'm glad I never met her."

"I didn't really know her either, although she was my dad's youngest sister. I heard them say once that she was married but after treating him badly had walked out, leaving her daughter behind. Then there was a second marriage, I believe after which she moved in with Aunt Harriet, supposedly pleading poverty, and my auntie, being so kind, fell for it. She was obviously a nightmare to live with, drove auntie to an early grave ."

"Didn't she then inherit all your Aunt Harriet's money?" asked James."

"Yes, and then what did she do? Sold the house, emptied the bank account and cleared off, and nobody knew where. We tried to let her know about mum's death," said Anna. Both with dad and mum we left a message with her previous neighbour. Anyway somehow she knew about Oakdene Manor hence the visits she made before mum had her stroke. She had tried her hardest to win mum over, but they really didn't get on. I think she stopped visiting after mum was taken ill, probably because she knew she was wasting her time.

"It's pretty obvious that she was angling for some of your dad's money," said James." I'm glad she didn't get any."

Chapter 3

James left Anna at the computer, put on his boots and jacket and called Jet, their black labrador. He ruffled his soft fur, receiving excited licks.

"Come on, boy. Time for a walk."

They'd bought Jet soon after moving to Oakdene Manor. It had been impossible in their former lives to have a dog, but now, times had changed. They'd a large house in the country and plenty of time for walks. Jet was a puppy in training, still boisterous but learning to respond to commands. James was firm with him. He rarely wore a lead except when any dangerous situation arose. The two of them were becoming well known in the village and Jet, like an aristocrat, permitted a certain amount of fuss from people that he knew.

They set off down the winding drive, Jet racing ahead to nose in the stream before James caught up with him. They then clattered over the narrow bridge, just wide enough for a reasonable sized van and passed through the stone gateway.

They turned right and strolled towards the first row of terraced houses, small cottages originally built for estate workers but now rented out to anybody who wanted to live in this quiet, isolated village on the slopes of the Cotswolds. The whole cluster of houses appeared very traditionally English. The big manor house beside the church, the sizeable, dilapidated rectory that would have been superb if the diocese had money to spend on it, the village green with ancient oak and horse chestnut trees surrounding a War Memorial dating from the First World war. A shop/Post Office selling almost everything stood opposite the school that had been closed because the pupil numbers had fallen and had been modernised into a very desirable dwelling.

There weren't many villagers about at this sunset hour. A few young people arriving home from work grabbing a bit of food from the shop that stayed open until late: some children riding about on bikes and old Joe, a retired jockey whose bandy legs creaked when he moved, still sitting outside his front door, prepared to talk to everyone who passed.

"Good evening Joe," said James. "Been another nice day."

Jet rushed over to the old man who stroked his soft head and accepted some friendly licks. These two seemed to adore each other and there was always a tasty morsel in Joe's pocket and a bowl of water by the door.

"--evening boss," said Joe touching his cap. He was very respectful to James and Anna because they lived in the big house. He knew everybody, just about, in the village. He was considered the biggest nosy parker or the wisest sage. James liked to think of him as the latter and would pick his brains about traditions and the history of the village.

Sadly the secrets of betrayal had passed Joe by. Nobody in the village it seems had suspected that anything untoward had been happening with the Manor and estate and when the revelation hit the newspapers they couldn't believe what they read. Their hearts had gone out to Anna and James, who had inherited this awful catastrophe, and if guardian angels were needed there would have been plenty of takers.

"Seems a lot more strangers in the village these days, driving through, making a noise. Two furniture vans today, people moving into the new estate, I suppose," said Joe.

"Yes, I expect so. I'm sorry about that," said James. Everyone knew that it was Oakdene land that had been sold, surreptitiously, by the suddenly departed owner's husband.

"It's all been a horrible revelation and I hope nothing more turns up to shock us," said James. He didn't want to discuss the happenings at the Manor. He knew that everything he said would be passed on by Joe who had nothing else to do but talk to people as they walked by. So he said," Come on Jet. Time to go."

Jet had made himself comfortable with his nose resting on Joe's boots. He only moved when the old man struggled to his feet.

"Time for a pint," he said, accepting a helping arm from James. They meandered along the pavement to the pub, *The Cat and Fiddle*. It was an inn, popular with the locals and Joe regularly met up with his cronies for a bite to eat and a frothing pint. He rarely missed, only staying at home if his gout was bad. Then the *old woman* from next door would bring him some of her vile broth or suet pudding. He knew he should be grateful but what with her helpfulness and his pain life became intolerable until he could escape from her again.

" Coming in?" asked Joe.

"No, another time. I must let Jet have a good walk. '--night, Joe."

James and Jet moved on along the village street to where they could see lights beginning to twinkle in the new houses that were being built behind the pub on land that had once been full of sheep. The estate seemed to be growing, the building still going on. It's not a bad thing, thought James, new houses, new people coming into the community. It was bound to happen. No small villages could expect to remain free of developers but it was Oakdene land that had been sold to them, unbeknown to Anna and James and there wasn't anything they could do about it now.

They crossed the street and walked across the village green towards a style set in the wall and a footpath that led down to the stream that eventually passed through the Manor garden. James climbed over it following Jet who had jumped through and was racing down to the water. It was only a shallow stream and he loved splashing in it. James always stayed clear when he came out and shook himself .Then they would follow the footpath along by the water which broadened out in places, passing through meadows that were once full of cows, but were now rampant with wild flowers, beautiful to see but farmland that was being wasted.

Unproductive, thought James, but not for much longer. He could see, in the distance scaffolding around Beeches farmhouse, left empty by the Marshal's, who had been suspected of being involved in stealing money and property from the estate. He and Anna were going through the seemingly endless task of hiring solicitors, detectives, going to court to try and sort out the problems with house and estate. An arrest had been made but the case against Stephen Marshall, the person in question had been lacking in evidence and he had been released. A year had passed since Celia's death and still the real person responsible had not been apprehended.

But the Marshal's had gone, unable to bear living there anymore and a new tenant was preparing to move into Beeches farm. James and Anna were spending what they could to do the house and barns up a bit. The fields had been neglected for a year, before that they had been sub let to other farmers and one had been turned into a caravan site. This now was empty, looking abandoned with bare patches and long grass showing where the caravans had stood, and a pile of bricks where the toilet and shower block had been. It was decided that they weren't needed so they had been demolished. However the stables and animal pens had been left where a prosperous little animal farm had existed for a short time.

They turned away from the stream, crossed a small wooden bridge and wandered back up the hill and across behind the church and churchyard. The church was small and very ancient, dedicated to St. Giles. Inside it was cool and had old box seats, a belfry with one bell and a beautiful stained glass window in the east end. Anna's mother had often played the tiny one manual organ for services when the regular organist couldn't. He had been an old man with bad arthritis and at times he could barely move his fingers.

James and Anna had started to go to the morning service on Sunday's. The congregation was small but were a faithful group that attended regularly. The rector, The Rev. Jones had two other small parishes to deal with as well.

There were a lot of graves in the churchyard, many with flowers decorating them. He looked towards where William and Celia were buried. Anna had replaced the flowers only yesterday. They made the churchyard seem bright and cheerful and the quiet peace was added to by the beauty of the stretching landscape beyond the wall.

There had been lots of grumbles apparently from locals about the noise, smoky barbecues and lack of respect for surrounding farms during the time that the caravan park had been open but, of course, it hadn't lasted very long. When the disaster at the manor occurred and Stephen Marshall had been accused of theft, the Marshall's had moved away and the caravan park closed.

Next to the church stood the old vicarage. Lucy Jones, the vicar's wife was in the garden watering her dahlias and on the bumpy lawn her two teenage sons were playing cricket. Suddenly a ball sailed over the fence and was immediately chased by Jet. James rescued it from his sharp teeth and threw it back.

"Thanks James," the boys shouted and then started arguing whether over the fence meant *out* or *a six*.

"Sorry about that," laughed Lucy, watching her offspring at play. "Nothing changes, they're cricket mad, and James answered, "It's nice to see them outside, playing, even if they do argue."

He and Jet tramped across the grass to the boundary wall, found a place they could climb over and wandered on through the parkland. It had seen tidier days. He'd a few retired men who came to work in the gardens. James paid them what he could but there was little money to spare. He knew that they were glad to help and made sure that they had a room in the outhouses to brew tea and rest their feet. They did a grand job, he had to admit, the shrubberies, orchard, flower beds were kept free of weeds and James was very grateful for their efforts. The walled vegetable garden was still flourishing. His mother-in-law, Celia had allowed villagers to have plots to work and they paid her with whatever they grew. James and Anna were glad to continue in the same way. There was a way in to this walled area from the road so the house, gardens and parkland were able to be kept private. *That would have suited Elliot, James thought.*

When they reached the house they went in through the back door. Jet splashed his water everywhere whilst quenching his raging thirst and James was also glad to settle down with a beer.

He wandered in to where Anna still sat at her Laptop.

"How's it going?" he asked.

"Well," I thought I'd found another painting," she said. It looked like the seascape that dad had of boats in Plymouth harbour but this one is for sale in Torquay and the reserved price is nowhere near what dad paid for his, so I don't believe that it's the same one. I always knew that dad's was a Turner but this painting has - unknown artist on it so it can't have been painted by him, can it?"

"Oh well. Keep trying. You never know Some of the remaining paintings may turn up, one day," said James. "Elliot didn't steal them to hang on a wall. He will sell them to the highest bidder for as much as he can. They are hot property and the chances are that he may be caught in the act especially if the sale is in this country. If he smuggles them abroad then they'll be much harder to find.

"Let's hope he doesn't then," said Anna.

Chapter 4

Anna didn't sleep well that night. The possibility of finding another of her dad's paintings had given her a real boost until she'd realised that it wasn't the valuable Turner that her dad had owned but a similar painting by an anonymous artist.

A few weeks ago the Police had returned the forgeries to her, after all they had been stolen from Oakdene Manor but she hadn't rehung them, even though the walls looked empty. The thought of looking at these reproductions every day made her feel sick, so they were bundled up in the loft, out of the way. She longed to set fire to them but knew that they were still evidence and could not be destroyed .

She longed to get the genuine ones back. There were still five extremely valuable paintings somewhere, she assumed in Elliot's possession and no doubt he'd been able to smuggle them out of the country. It was unlikely that he wouldn't have escaped abroad as soon as he could, but how he'd managed to take the paintings with him was a mystery. She tossed about, trying not to disturb James but could not settle. She knew, in her heart of hearts that it would be difficult - well almost impossible that any of them would be found and she realised, finally that they could be anywhere in the world by now.

Still lying sleepless she transferred her thoughts to the difficult time following her father's funeral. James had stayed on until the end of the week. Her mother had needed help organising the immediate legal requirements that followed a death. They had gone to the solicitor's with her and had made a start on going through her father's papers and files. Her dad had died so suddenly that there had been many things to deal with. However he had left a straightforward will leaving everything to her mum and then, on her death, to herself.

Fortunately they'd been ably helped by David, the

estate manager. He'd previously been her dad's right hand man when running his estate agencies in the West Country and had been persuaded to come to live and work for him at Oakdene. It had been just as easy to administer his other businesses from there. Her dad had decided, however, that as he was in semi retirement he would sell or close down many of his business ventures and properties and concentrate on the Oakdene estate.

He'd changed one of the old out buildings that had been formerly used as sleeping quarters for servants, and storage for stable equipment, and had also created an estate office with a flat upstairs. Here David had settled quite happily. He was a single man, not overly tall with a mop of black hair and had a very friendly personality. Her mum had spoilt him with tasty cakes, pies etc. and treated him almost like the son she had never had. There was no doubt that he had been devastated by her dad's sudden death and not sure where his future now lay.

Anna and Adam had stayed for a few more weeks with her mum as it was the summer holidays. Earlier in the year they'd booked what should have been a relaxing family holiday, to Tenerife, but had felt forced to cancel it. It had been too soon to leave her mum on her own and anyway Anna knew that she wouldn't have enjoyed it. She missed her dad so much. So with no holiday, James had come back, taking his fortnight's leave to help with her mum's inheritance of Oakdene Manor.

Adam had been too young to mind about missing his seaside holiday. He loved it at Oakdene, but had found it difficult to understand why his grandad was no longer there.

James and Anna had studied with David, bank statements, investment portfolios, property owned and rented, the extent of the estate lands and the value of Oakdene manor, its paintings and contents. It all amounted to a vast sum, much of which, would go to the tax man. However Anna's mum had been left a very wealthy woman and this had caused them to worry. As it had turned out they had been right to do so. No-one could have believed the scheming and consequent result that had occurred during her mum's illness and after her death.

It had been hard for Anna to leave her mother and return home and to school. but her mum had put on a brave face.

"I'll be fine Anna," she'd said. "You're not far away and we'll speak every day on the phone. I've got Hazel, the dogs, my book club friends, and golfing partners. I'll make sure I keep busy. Anyway David is just across the yard."

This had all sounded positive but to Anna the Manor, her childhood home was a large rambling, now empty house which would stimulate many memories. How was her mother going to cope when finding herself alone during the dark winter nights?

Finally they'd left, with the assurance that they would be up every weekend they could and would ring or text every day. Anna hadn't been able to hold back the tears when she had looked back at the solitary figure of her mother, standing outside the front door, waving them goodbye, and as they'd rumbled over the bridge James had said, "She'll survive. She's a lot stronger than you think."

"I know," she'd sniffed, "but I hate leaving her on her own."

Hazel had promised to keep a very close eye on her and Anna had known that she was to be relied on, but it hadn't stopped her worrying and it had been extremely difficult for her to say goodbye to her mother.

Time had, however, passed and to Anna's delight her mum had not only survived the winter but seemed to have taken on a new lease of life. Anna knew that her parents had been very happy together, but now her dad had gone, she had been worried that her mum would fall into a miserable decline at the prospect of being alone.

Fortunately she'd started off positively trying to organise every minute of the day so that her mind was well occupied and not constantly lingering on the past.

Anna had been so relieved at how busy her mum had become. She had made it her duty to visit her tenants, regularly, and enjoyed looking around their farms and having tea in their cosy farmhouse kitchens. She had started teaching piano to two little girls who loved to come and play her big grand piano.

She had suggested that the kitchen garden surrounded by a wall be carved into allotments for anyone who wanted to use them, her only rent being some produce when it was plentiful.

Hazel and Jenny had become good friends and to Jenny's children Oakdene Manor had become like a second home. There were so many paths to cycle along and lots of grass to kick a ball on. She knew that her mum loved to see them, wishing that Adam could have lived a bit nearer to join in.

So although she missed Anna's dad terribly, her mum had settled down to a busy life, knowing that he'd approve of her forging forward and keeping everything going just as he would have done.

Having eventually dropped off to sleep Anna woke up the next morning surprisingly bright-eyed. Shifting James wasn't quite such an easy matter. This semi-retirement had made him lazy.

"Come on, get up, James," she said, shaking him.

She was met with a groan.

"What's the time?" he asked.

"7.30."

"Why so early?"

"We're sorting out the office buildings and outhouses. Remember!"

"Oh, is that all? There's plenty of time. I'll get up in a minute then I'll have to take Jet for a walk."

"I'll make a start then but don't take all morning doing that."

Anna left him pretending to get up and went down stairs for her breakfast. Jet got all excited when he saw her and they romped about for a while with a squeaky toy. It seemed like a bright morning outside so she opened the back door and let him out. After some cereal and toast she fed Jet then went back upstairs to get dressed. James had turned over and nodded off again so she made a clatter as she opened drawers .

"Alright, you've made your point," he grumbled and sat up, yawned, stretched and searched for his slippers.

Anna put on some old clothes and went back downstairs to the kitchen.

The outbuildings and disused office had lain derelict for months and she knew that they would be dusty and full of junk. Their first priority when they had moved in had been the house. Instead of working in the estate office James had taken over her dad's study and anything to do with the estate had been transferred there.

She remembered her mother's phone call the night she told her that David had handed in his notice. He'd stayed for about three months after her dad's death, finalised all necessary business and made sure that everything to do with the estate was organised so that her mum could understand it or explain things to a new estate manager.

David's leaving had left a great gap in her mum's life. She had been upset, but understood why he'd decided to go. He had missed her dad greatly. They had got on so well together. There was no joy for him at Oakdene any more, no challenge, so he'd applied and was given a job in the head office of Thomas Wood's housing development company and would be working in Bristol where his family lived and where he had grown up. He had kept in touch with her mum, until she died. He had also met again and married an old time girlfriend, Hannah, and was now the father of two boys.

So her mum had been left alone in a large house surrounded by a vast estate and with a massive fortune in the Bank. This had been a worrying factor for Anna and James but they had chosen, because of commitments, to ignore their worries and go along with what the future unveiled - an error of judgement they would, sadly, live to regret.

Chapter Five

Anna took a bunch of keys from a hook by the door and slipping on some shoes walked across the yard to the old office building. The stable yard had originally been cobbled but, in many places these had been replaced with slabs. Even so it wasn't easy to walk on. The back part of the house formed one side of the yard and the other three were made up of horse stalls, grooms quarters, store rooms as well as the old office building. Now they were all rapidly falling into disrepair. In the fifteen years since her dad's death very little maintenance had been done. David, of course, had not stayed to see that the place was kept in order and her mum had done her best but was glad to hand it all over to Elliot when he arrived in her life.

Anna unlocked the door of the old estate office and pushed it open. She walked in past the stairs that led up to the flat and through into the office itself, imagining how it had once been with David and her dad sitting facing each other at their central desks discussing estate and other business. Now the desks were bare, the shelves empty and dusty. James had cleared and taken away anything that had been left, which wasn't much, and now, of course did all the estate business from his study in the manor house.

Anna turned and climbed the stairs to the upstairs flat. She peeped into all the rooms, the small sitting room, bedroom, bathroom and kitchen. All the furniture was still there from the time that David had occupied it but it looked shabby and the whole place felt damp. It wouldn't do. It would all have to go. She'd enjoy fitting it out with something new. She had come up with the idea of making these empty buildings into holiday cottages. They'd found an architect who was in the process of drawing up some plans. It was likely to be costly but lots of stately homes etc. were doing this kind of thing and it could bring in a useful amount of money to bolster the estates funds.

All the money from the sale of their house in Bristol

was being spent on this project. They had already used up their savings on repairs to the Manor. Her dad had done the same when he'd bought the house in 1985, and the roof and walls etc. were still fine but the bathrooms had needed modernising and everywhere had required decoration. Their own furniture had found a new home also. So much was missing of the original furnishings that her own few bits easily fitted in.

The next door she opened was an old food store. Some rungs had been set in the wall and were the only means of climbing through a trap door into the loft above. Once up there instead of a window there was a wide wooden door that opened to a perilous drop to the yard. Hay or straw would have been stored up there and pitchforked down into a cart in the yard below.

Next to this were the horse stalls with their doors cut in half, (Adam's description when he was a boy). Her mother had looked after some horses there for Lucille, but of course was unable to continue once she'd had her stroke. Now they stood empty with a fusty smell. Turning the corner were some open covered areas where farm vehicles had been kept and now housed their own cars. Above were some upstairs rooms which would make an apartment and some stairs going up to a room above the archway entrance to the yard. This would give the apartment some character.

On the other side of the archway was a mess room used now by the old gardeners. It contained a chipped Belfast sink, chairs and tables and was a good watering hole for the two old men who kindly kept the gardens tidy. However this room would have to be incorporated in her new scheme. She'd find a warmer, more comfortable place for them within the many disused back parts of the house.

James had joined her by the time she'd got to the last and biggest outhouse. This was where he kept his ride-on mower- his new piece of essential equipment that was only for his use (and not for the gardeners!)

He pulled open the double doors and switched on the

lights. Dust swirled in the rays of the sun and caused a misty haze over the piles of junk that had gradually piled up. It all had to go, but first there was a lot of sorting to be done, in case there was anything of value that was still there.

"Here we go then," said James moving his precious mower out of the way. "You make a start and I'll help when I've taken Jet for a quick walk."

Anna looked around assessing what had been dumped there. She was quite excited, hoping to find all sorts of interesting things. She started moving out a few smaller items and when James returned they piled them in different categories in the yard. There was a lot of wood - broken chairs, tables, a small ladder and an old wheelbarrow plus lots of boards, planks and broken boxes. Most of this was useless and could be chopped up and burned. Metal such as battered buckets without handles, an old tin bath with a hole in, a variety of rusty tools, and old vehicle wheels were put in another pile and would have to be taken to the tip. It wasn't long before Anna realised that there was nothing there worth saving. It was definitely no Aladdin's cave. A certain person had made sure of that.

They found piles of newspapers that had been nibbled by mice, ropes hanging from hooks on the ceiling that had become a framework for spiders. There was a box full of broken china and tyres from a variety of vehicles leant against the walls. A few old coats, blankets and rugs were strewn about and empty picture frames, some with broken glass and piles of books were leant against the walls. The worst part about the whole place was the rubbish. Piles of stones, bricks, paper bags, empty boxes and food tins, junk of every description all left as a parting gesture. James and Anna had known that it would be a tough job to clear this place and had left it until now as there had been so many more urgent jobs to do.

The yard was full by the time they had finished emptying. There were piles of black bags and the old bath was full of broken glass, as well as there being heaps of wood, metal, bricks and stones.

There were a few items that Anna had salvaged. Some large clay pots, the old wheelbarrow and a rusty mangle. She wanted to break up the severity of the yard and had already put some geraniums in an old stone water trough. It would be lovely if she could put a few trees in large containers in the middle and various groups of pots with flowers in outside the cottage doors. The mangle could be a feature too and the old wheelbarrow could be painted and filled with flowers.

Ideas danced around her head as she helped James load the Land Rover with black bags and old sacks filled with junk.

"This will take me the rest of the day," he grumbled as he set off for the tip which was a fair distance on the outskirts of Cheltenham.

Jack, one of the gardeners turned up just as he was leaving.

"I'll chop up this wood, gaffer," he said. "Some of it will make good kindling."

"Thanks, Jack," said James, "but I think most of it is only good for a bonfire. I'll see you later."

As James drove off Anna showed Jack the now empty building. It felt very cold inside and as she swept the floor she realised it was made of slabs.

"Used to be a dairy," said Jack."The floor had to be cold. They'd keep the milk here in churns ready for market and they'd make butter and cream.'-- Pity there's nothing left but you can see where a stone sink stood over yonder.-- I'll get on with that wood then Mrs., "said Jack and ambled off to fetch a chopper.

"Thanks," said Anna as she went to fetch some water to throw on the dusty floor. It would make sweeping easier. She'd already tied a scarf around her mouth but the air filled with years of undisturbed dust made her cough and sneeze. There wasn't much point in overdoing it. The whole place would be renovated, so she left the doors open to let in air and went back to the kitchen to clean herself up.

She was well pleased with her morning's work. When James came back they'd have a late lunch and then she'd help him load up the car again for another trip to the tip.

At the end of this first year things were looking up. James had fathomed out all the finances, such as they were. The devastating truth had been hard to face. They only had the value of Oakdene Manor and parkland. Everything else had been stolen from them.

However, the house now sparkled with fresh paint and her big new plan for the cottages was beginning to take shape. Adam would be home soon from university. He was doing environmental studies at Bristol, was an enthusiastic member of the Green Party, had been on several marches protesting about a variety of threats to the countryside and was very keen to help with the estate lands. He intended to draw up a detailed map of their property, estate and farmlands and take note of how it was used .

In a few weeks time he would arrive with his friend Jason, both eager to work. After all Oakdene was Adam's inheritance, too, and he intended to work and make it prosper. He was bringing Jason, as his parents lived abroad. Jason's father was a diplomat and moved from one British embassy to another. Jason usually went to visit them at Christmas and they would come over in the summer. They had bought a small house for him on the outskirts of Bristol that Adam now shared. The two had met at a lecture on badger culling as Jason was training to be a vet, and become good friends.

Anna was looking forward to their arrival. A couple of lively young men about the place would be like a breath of fresh air.

She prepared the lunch then sat in the old comfy chair to wait for James.

She was disappointed not to have found anything worth salvaging in amongst the junk but she hadn't really been surprised. The whole house had been systematically gone through and they had no-one to blame but themselves. When her mum had been moved to the nursing home Anna had put her trust in others, and this trust had been badly abused. Their lives had been career orientated and seeing to her mother and young son had been Anna's priority. She had believed the Manor to be in good hands and had had promises that it would be looked after. As to the future, well it had been something she hadn't wanted to think about until the time, a few days after her mum's funeral when they had walked in through the front door and discovered ----.

They had been horrified at the desecration, the systematic removing of everything of value, that included, of course, her father's valuable paintings.

Chapter Six

When James came in Anna was curled up in the old kitchen chair, fast asleep.

"Aha, caught napping," he laughed, giving her a peck on the cheek.

"I'll not hug you. I'm filthy."

He went to the sink and started scrubbing his hands clean, then splashed his face. He gulped down a glass of water and collapsed onto a chair at the table.

"I seem to be permanently dirty and exhausted these days."

"But it's rewarding work, isn't it, seeing what we've done - having ideas for the future? It feels like there's hope, like a light at the end of the tunnel," said Anna, as she placed the food on the table.

"Don't get too carried away," said James. "We're practically penniless, will soon have spent our last bit of cash and then we'll have to borrow. I'll probably have to go back to work. The police don't seem to be treating our case with any urgency. Finding the real culprits is the only chance of getting our money back, what's left of it, and as for your mum's valuables the longer they are missing the harder they will be to find."

"It's a pity about the painting that I thought I'd discovered," she said, feeling annoyed. They ate their salad and jacket potatoes in silence. Neither of them relished the idea of chasing criminals but when something or someone of your own becomes threatened then there is no other recourse but to fight back.

Anna poured out some tea.

"Any cake left"? asked James.

"A little," said Anna. "You've eaten most of it."

"Well it is very good. You should make some more."

Anna smiled, feeling very pleased. Now she had the time she'd started to try out a few recipes. After all, there were some exceptionally good bakers amongst the village community, all eager to give her tips.

"Well this won't do. I'd better get on and fill the Land Rover again ."

"Shall I help?"

"No, no, I'll get Jack."

"Alright, If you're sure."

With James gone Anna went into the lounge and sat down at the piano. She strummed away at some Ivor Novello songs. She'd bought a book on the Internet after watching *Gosford Park* on the TV. Her mother's piano was one of the large pieces of furniture that had remained in the house. It's very size and weight were its salvation as it needed careful treatment and a lot of men to move it.

As she played she glanced at the elegant bureau standing under the window. This had been her mother's and surprisingly also left behind. It was made of a rich, deep mahogany, with delicate curved legs. Presumably it had been left because one of the legs had been broken and it had fallen lopsided onto the floor.

"It's received some rough treatment," James had said, as he'd propped it up on some books, but they hadn't been surprised at the state of it because every drawer had been gone through and the contents left spilled across the floor.

He'd mended it, as best he could, but it was fragile. Fortunately they didn't need to use it much now. All the household paper work was kept in a filing cabinet in the study.

On the bureau had stood a framed photo of her mother on her wedding day, smiling up at her new husband. They'd found it on the floor with the glass smashed. Anna had given it to the Police. Elliot had not allowed many photos of himself to be taken. *No need to wonder why,* she thought. Her mother had looked very happy, and she was glad that she had known nothing about what her husband had done. She had been so trusting and content with him, but sadly, been so badly taken in. Elliot had been ten years younger than her, and that in itself should have been a cause for concern. His photo showed a tall, good looking man with a mop of greying hair and a beard. *He's probably changed his looks now,* she thought, maybe *by dyeing his hair and shaving off his beard.*

She stopped playing and looked at the photo that she had put in its place, one of her mother with the two dogs. It had been when she had gone out walking them one day that her mum had first met Elliot.

This encounter had taken place about a couple of years after her dad's death. Anna had been relieved that her mother had seemed so settled. They'd visited her as much as they could and she had come to stay with them quite frequently bringing the dogs as well, which pleased Adam. However, quite often, in their phone calls she had started to mention a man called Elliot.

"Who is he?" Anna had asked.

"Oh, he's the friend who helped me with Bonnie."

About a month before this conversation her mum had rung up in a very distressed state and said that Bonnie, her little dog, had died.

"What happened?" Anna had asked.

"Well we went for a walk after tea and he just stopped and lay down," she had said, sniffing. "I pulled his lead and said," Come on Bonnie, we're nearly home, but he wouldn't move. I knelt down, on the pavement, to stroke him and realised that he wasn't breathing and that his eyes were wide open. I couldn't believe that he had just laid down and died. I pulled Mitzy away as she was sniffing around Bonnie wondering why he was lying so still."

Anna had heard her mother sobbing.

"Mum, mum, shall I come up?" she had said.

"No, it's alright. I was so upset,--- for a moment I didn't know what to do. I sat on a wall and stroked Mitzy. I was sobbing. I couldn't help it. It was getting dark and you know there's never any body about, but suddenly a car did come by, stopped, and a man got out and hurried across the road.

"Has he been knocked down? Was it a hit and run?" he had said.

"I told him that Bonnie had just fallen," she had said, crying again, "and that he wouldn't get up."

"Let's get him to a vet," the man had said.

"It's too late for that," she had cried. "He's dead."

"Even so, we'll take him. The vet needs to examine him to see why he died so suddenly."

"So this kind man had fetched a blanket, wrapped up poor Bonnie and carried him to his car. The vet had said that Bonnie'd had a heart attack and there had been nothing much he or anybody could have done, so, sadly, we brought him home and Elliot dug a hole and we buried him in the garden near the roses. Oh, Anna it's so quiet without him," her mother had said, " and poor Mitzy keeps wandering about searching, trying to find him. He's another memory of your dad that is gone."

"We're coming up for half-term in a couple of weeks, " Anna had said. "Then perhaps we can meet this man and thank him."

Anyway during that two weeks Elliot's name had cropped up in nearly every phone call between Anna and her mother. He had called the next day to see how her mum was and she had asked him in for tea. They'd then arranged to meet once or twice a week to take Mitzy for a walk.

He'd also noticed several jobs about the place that needed doing, like oiling the squeaky back door, unbunging a drain, fixed a rattling window etc. and it was obvious that to Celia he was becoming indispensible.

"The sooner we meet him the better," James had said. He'd originally decided not to visit with Anna and Adam at halfterm, being so busy at work, but had changed his mind and rearranged his appointments. There was no way he was staying at home. This new Lothario needed to be inspected.

"Let's hope he is a genuinely nice bloke," James had said, "and not a gold digger. Celia is a very wealthy widow."

"I know, but surely he wouldn't --- "Anna had replied.

" -- take her for all she's got. Who knows, but be careful, Anna," James had said. "If he's charmed your mother he could do the same to you."

"Oh, don't be silly James. I'm not that gullible."

"Well, we shall see."

Anna replaced the photo and stood, looking out of the window remembering the Saturday of half-term that they'd arrived at Oakdene Manor and been told that Elliot had been invited to join them for dinner.

He had come, dressed casually in an open necked shirt and light grey trousers, obviously determined to impress. He had helped carry dishes, pull out chairs for Anna and Celia at the table before sitting down himself and afterwards had sat on the floor playing cars with Adam.

They hadn't been able to fault him but, of course they'd discovered later that he was very used to moving in influential circles and knew all there was to know about charming the ladies. James had pumped him for information, trying not to make it too obvious but after all, Anna had a right to know something about the man that her mother was welcoming into her home.

"Are you staying somewhere around here, Elliot?" he'd asked.

"Yes, with my son," he'd replied. He's just taken over one of the farms here on the Oakdene estate. I spend my time, now between him and my brother, Douglas, who lives in Bristol. Douglas is on his own, like me and there's so much to do there. It's great having the time to visit. He's an artist and we go to a lot of exhibitions. In fact he rang today wanting me to come back and go to one with him in Oxford so, I thought, as you're here with your mum that I would go down and stay for a while."

Anna had seen her mother's face drop although she'd tried to hide it and she'd also seen James smirk a little and nod his head.

It was obvious that Celia hadn't expected him to leave so soon and it was a realisation to them all that Elliot was a free spirit, not tied down by anyone or anything, and could come and go as he pleased.

Anna remembered the comment James had made, as they had prepared for bed.

"So, as soon as we arrive, he departs. Let's hope there isn't an omen in that. It looks as though your mum's got to accept that he'll be away as much as he's around."

"Perhaps it means that he is above board," Anna had replied. If he wasn't he'd be sniffing around here all the time."

"Mm, I'm not so sure, "James had said. "I think we are going to have to keep a very close watch on the situation."

He had been right, so right, but, as things turned out they had forgotten this piece of wisdom until it was too late.

Chapter Seven

Anna left the lounge and wandered along the passage to the kitchen. Jet stirred from his basket and with his energy restored started leaping around her wagging his tail.

She looked outside and seeing that James hadn't yet returned said, "Come on Jet. We'll go for a wander."

They made their way across the stable yard, passed under the archway then turned right and progressed through the rose garden. Ahead of them the sweeping lawn stretched across to the small copse that hid the road and it's noisy traffic. She sat on an old garden seat and looked at the manor settled so serenely in its Cotswold setting with the late afternoon sun shining on the mullioned windows. It was a large, sprawling but wonderfully charismatic building with a huge lounge, dining room and study and a comfortable old kitchen with many passages and storage rooms that stretched across the back of the house. Upstairs were six bedrooms and three bathrooms above which a series of attics, one leading from another, each with a dormer window, lay empty except for the few things that they had put in them, including the fake paintings.

What a legacy, she thought, and to think I nearly lost it all.

She watched as Jet snuffled around locating different smells and thought again about the half-term holiday when they had met Elliot for the first time, during which he had mentioned that he was going to stay with his brother for a few weeks.

It had seemed a little rude if not strange that he'd decided to leave just as they had arrived, so before they went home at the end of the week, they decided to do, without her mum's knowledge, one or two things that would make them feel more comfortable.

They had gone round the house listing everything that they considered valuable, or collectable. It was a sobering exercise as there seemed to be so much. The list included the paintings. Her dad had bought six originals that must have cost him a fortune. James had found out, to his relief, from William's solicitor that he had left details of each one with him along with information and photographs about some of the jewellery that he had bought for Celia.

Even so their own list had included items of silver, bone china, ornaments, some elegant small pieces of furniture, rugs and many expensive items of clothing. They had felt bad about snooping but the situation with Elliot had forced their hand. Anna's mum was a woman of fortune and a great catch to any prospective suitor.

"It isn't that we want every penny for ourselves, or in the future for Adam," Anna had said. "It's just that dad worked very hard for this, so why should anyone with criminal intentions think that they can steal it."

"Yes, but it could happen," said James, "and that's why we've got to be prepared."

Elliot had returned from his visit to his brother that had lasted three weeks. Her mum, had sounded very excited on the phone.

"He's brought me a lovely bunch of lilies and roses, Anna."

It appeared from then on that he was to become a daily visitor. They had started to go out together to the theatre, cinema, for meals, days out with the dog, and Anna had to admit that if her mother was happy and not alone, then it was a great relief to her.

Her mum had also been to meet Elliot's family at Beeches farm, had been invited to dinner and was beginning to get to know them quite well.

"His son, Stephen's a bit dour," she had said to Anna, but his new wife, Lucille is the exact opposite. She made me very welcome. She's very glamorous for a farmer's wife. I don't think she does much on the farm but she keeps a few horses and walks about in jodhpurs all day. I think she'd like a more elevated position in society, tries to speak all lah-de-dah, but really she's very friendly."

"I wonder why," said James, cynically, when he heard.

Suddenly her mum had seemed to have become indispensible especially to Lucille. She helped in the stables with the horses and held the reins for young riders that Lucille was teaching.

"She wants to own some stables one day and run a proper riding school," her mum had said. "I'm wondering whether to offer her the use of our stables here. They're just standing empty, but there's only room for about three horses. I could help look after them. It would give me an interest."

Anna had seen the logic in that but wasn't sure if it was all above board. However she was not her mother's guardian and didn't live near enough to really know what exactly went on. Her mum's frequent chatter on the phone was her only feedback and the occasional visits that she and James made. Often these days, when they suggested visiting, her mother would say that she was busy or going out for the day with Elliot.

The months had passed with Elliot still making his occasional visits to his brother.

"It would seem that mum doesn't have much time for us these days," Anna had said to James. "I'd be happy if I didn't have a horrible feeling, at the back of my mind that Elliot and his family are just too good to be true."

Anna thought she heard James returning and, calling to Jet made her way back to the courtyard. She looked around but there was no sign of him. It must have been some other vehicle passing, she thought. She looked round the yard There was still plenty of clearing to do. Over to one side was the pile of wood waiting to be burnt. Amongst it was a dried out Christmas tree.

This reminded her of their first Christmas with Elliot. Before Anna had mentioned it her mum had broached the subject.

"You will come up and stay, won't you? I've asked Elliot and his family over on Christmas Day. It'll be great having a house full again."

So that had been it. The decision made. Christmas with the Marshall's.

"Lovely!" James had said sarcastically.

"Well the more we get to know them the better," Anna had said.

"It'll be great," Adam had said." I like Elliot. He's funny."

"So he's gradually winning everyone over," James had said sceptically, and Anna had been glad that he'd kept her reined in. It was hard to think badly of people. They might be completely honest, but the niggle was still there. *Who was Elliot? What was he after and was Lucille the good friend that she made out to be?*

Her mother had started to lead a very busy life. She looked after the horses, learnt how to groom them. Helped with the young riders. She had bought some jodhpurs to wear, like Lucille. They went shopping together, out for coffee with friends and many times she'd invite these friends back to Oakdene Manor which they didn't fail to admire.

"Nothing surprising about that," Anna had said to James.

They hadn't been able to visit for long at Christmas. It had been a busy, strenuous term. Anna, now deputy head seemed to be doing two jobs, not one. She'd managed to get presents organised, a Bristol city football strip for Adam and some football boots. All he seemed to want to do was kick a ball about with his friends. James was always happy with books and her mother, perfumes, bath fragrances, anything to help preserve her ageing skin.

However, this year they'd had to buy something for the Marshals. You couldn't spend Christmas Day with someone without giving them a present.

"Spirits and chocolates should do it," James had said. "I'll organise it when I go looking for something for my mother."

James' mother, Maud, had lived with his sister in Newent, a small town outside Gloucester, in her latter years and they'd visited her as often as they could until she'd died a few years ago.

Anna had been surprised that instead of feeling uncomfortable with her mother's new friends she'd really enjoyed their company. She thought that she might have felt like a stranger in her own home but, in fact, it had been quite the opposite.

They'd travelled up on the 23rd and stayed until the 30th as they'd been invited to a party organised by a school colleague on New Year's Eve and she was really looking forward to that.

When they'd arrived the house and tree had already been decorated.

"Lucille had thought it would be a lovely welcome for Adam," her mum had said , "but we've left one or two baubles for him to hang on the lower branches."Anna had suggested that they opened presents early on Christmas Day.

"You can't make a young boy wait until everyone's arrived."

It had been fun sitting round the tree, fishing out parcels from underneath, seeing Adam's excitement especially with his boots and kit.

But then, after breakfast they'd started preparing the Christmas dinner scheduled to be eaten about 2 o' clock.

It was always a joy being back in the familiar old kitchen helping her mother prepare all the traditional Christmas food.

"I've got trifle as well as Christmas pudding," her mum had said. "There's a lot of us to feed this year,--- and ice cream of course for my special grandson."

She had given Adam a hug as he sat on a stool whilst his father laced up his new boots ready for a kick around.

"Thanks, Granny," he'd said returning the hug before dashing outside.

About one o clock the guests had knocked on the back

door and hurried into the warmth carrying a large bag of presents. Adam had hurled himself on to Elliot who'd swung him up in the air, giving him a big hug.

"What a welcome," her mum had said as she'd introduced Adam to Stephen and Lucille, ---"and this is my daughter Anna and her husband, James." There had been kisses and handshakes all round.

Christmas dinner had been a great success, the food eaten with relish, many a bottle of good wine downed and afterwards they'd opened the rest of the presents.

Elliot's present to Adam had been a train set which James and Stephen set up on the hall floor.

Anna, her mum and Lucille had settled in armchairs to sip coffee and watch the Queen's speech. Happy banter and arguments had wafted in from the hall as Stephen, James and Adam had sorted out the train set.

Anna had suddenly felt a tug on her arm. It had been Adam saying, "Come on, mummy -- come and see."

They had gone into the hall where Stephen and James were stretched out watching the trains go round. They seemed to be getting on very well whilst Elliot sat on the settle constructing the station.

"Your turn Adam," Stephen had said, climbing to his feet. "We musn't take over, eh James."

"I suppose not," James had conceded, smiling. "Anyway," he'd said. "It's time to take Mitzy for a walk, before it gets too dark. Anyone want to come," he'd asked, as he put the lead on the excited dog?

Both Elliot and Stephen grabbed their coats, put on their shoes and plunged out into the murky cold. Adam had been left playing, happily with his trains.

The three women had started to clear and wash up.

"It was a superb meal," Lucille had said to Celia as she'd scrubbed pans in the sink and so nice to be amongst such good company."

She'd sounded so genuine that Anna's resolve to be hostile had gradually faded away. She'd understood how welcome and comfortable her mum had felt on meeting Lucille and she'd had to admit that Elliot appeared to adore her.

"Perhaps we've been too quick to judge them," she'd said later, to James. "They seem perfectly normal caring people."

"I have to agree," James had said. "Stephen opened up on our walk about his ideas for the farm whilst Elliot talked only of your mum."

So it had been no surprise to them when, a few months later her mother had told them that she and Elliot were to be married.

Chapter Eight

James was back. He drove into the courtyard, stopped the car and got out. He walked in through the back door looking exhausted and fed up.

"Well, I'm not going there again. I'll hire a skip, if needs be," he said.

"Why, what happened?" asked Anna.

"Well, when I got there the man in charge was about to close the gates. I got out and asked him to let me in. He was extremely objectionable, said they closed at 3.30. So I said that I'd been driving for half an hour, had a car full of all sorts of rubbish and was certainly not taking it back again. He wasn't happy but let me in. I said it'd be quicker if he helped. He was a lazy, overweight bloke and did so, begrudgingly, at his own pace, so I took my time. It didn't bother me that he was delayed in closing up when it was only halfway through the afternoon. I've a good mind to write to the council and complain but I don't suppose they'd take any notice."

"Well, never mind, at least you did manage to get the car emptied. Why don't you go and have a shower while I make the tea," said Anna, hustling James towards the hall door.

As she moved around the kitchen she sighed, realising that she really must do some housework. The floor was looking very grimy as usual because of the dog's muddy feet and James's mucky boots. Even though there were only the two of them, Oakdene Manor was a very large house and there was always a lot to be done.

Years ago Hazel, who lived in the village, had kept it spotless for her mum but around the time of her dad's death she had started to suffer from arthritis and Jenny, her daughter had taken over. After David had left, Hazel's husband, Barry, newly retired, had also offered to help by working in the estate office.

When Elliot came on the scene, Barry had been glad to

pass the estate work onto him as he needed to be at home a lot more to look after Hazel.

The mixed grill was about ready when James came down looking cleaner and seeming calmer. As they ate they talked about the holiday cottage project.

"The final plans and costing should come in soon," said James. "Roger Watson's being a bit slow, if you ask me -- and then we'll have to wait probably for months for planning permission. No-one seems to get on with things these days."

"The courtyard will look so different," said Anna. "Do you remember when mum kept some of Lucille's horses here? They really brought the place to life and it was lovely for Adam, when we visited."

When they had finished their tea Anna washed up whilst James took himself off to the computer. Then she made some coffee and carried it into the lounge. She sat down and took a photo album from a shelf.

It contained pictures of her mum's wedding to Elliot. She opened it and there she was, her mum, looking radiantly happy. *How cruel life can be*, she thought that someone like her mum could be hoodwinked by a man who appeared to care and be utterly devoted, yet had turned out in reality to be nothing but a money-grabbing, rogue.

She ought to shut the book and not punish herself but instead she continued to turn the pages.

The wedding had been in late August, still in the school holidays. Her mother had looked very elegant in a cream, lacy suit with a fetching wispy hat. Elliot, in morning dress had seemed every bit the glamorous husband. To anyone who didn't know the difference in their ages the ten years gap seemed completely unnoticeable. Her mother had always been slim and kept her hair stylishly coloured and Elliot, although younger had shown quite a lot of grey in his. So they appeared well matched.

James, with Stephen and Elliot's brother, Douglas, had worn dress suits and Adam, at the age of eight wore a smaller version. Tears came into Anna's eyes as she looked at her smart, young son. He had been so excited, had never been to a wedding before and he'd enjoyed every minute.

It had been the one and only time that Anna and James had seen Douglas. In fact they had been surprised that he'd accepted the wedding invitation at all. Many times when Elliot had visited him Celia had said, "Ask him to come and stay with us. We live in a beautiful part of the country. He could paint to his heart's content," but the invitation had never been taken up, that is if Elliot had ever passed the message on. Douglas had remained just a person in name only until his unexpected appearance at his brother's wedding.

He had not stayed long, refusing the offer of accommodation at the Manor and returned home that same evening. He had appeared pleasant enough although had little to say. He was shorter than Elliot and a little stockier but had the same look, the same unreadable expression that so baffled those who met him.

Now, with understanding, Anna realised that he hadn't wanted to become involved with them or be questioned because he knew that the whole event of the marriage was a sham and he had only accepted the invitation because it would have appeared strange if he had refused it. To the family, the brothers had seemed very close but their closeness was not only that of relationship but evolved around the plot that the two of them were masterfully planning.

Celia and Elliot had been married in the village church of St. Giles, the same church that had held the funeral service for her dad. Anna had remembered thinking that he would have approved. He wouldn't have wanted her mum to be on her own for the rest of her life.

After photographs they'd returned to the manor house for the reception. Caterers had taken over and the place had looked splendid.

Elliot had been an Oscar winning actor that day. His

speech had been honeyed and slick, making Celia blush and others gasp at the Shakespearian lyricism that flowed from his lips. Nobody had known that this was just an example of the way he had journeyed through life, mixing with the aristocracy and helping the richer members of society to spend their fortunes.

Stephen, as best man, nervously stood up and told the company how happy he was that his father had come back into his life and that he hoped, now he was married to Celia, that they would enjoy many happy years working together.

Elliot had sat back, smiled, joined in the toasts and held her mum's hand, later whispering in her ear that it was time to go.

Their bags had already been packed for a three week honeymoon in the South of France and they had left straight after the reception driving to London to stay overnight before flying to Nice airport.

It had been a joyous farewell on what had been such a happy day. There had been kisses all round, handshakes, plenty of confetti scattered and they had all raced to the gate to wave the happy couple off. Anna, suddenly feeling tearful had been glad of James' strong arm around her as they'd turned to go back up the drive.

Gradually the guests had left and when the caterers had finished tidying up, Anna and James with Stephen and Lucille had relaxed over a welcome coffee in the lounge.

Oakdene Manor was to be locked up for the duration of the honeymoon. Lucille, dressed in a body-clinging dress of colourful chiffon (that James had called outrageous, but nevertheless a focus for his attention) had previously taken the horses back to the farm temporarily, and Jenny had been given a key to prepare the house for Elliot and her mum's return.

Anna, James and Adam had gone home the next day but by then the euphoria had evaporated and the worry had, once again, started to invade Anna's thoughts. Her mother was now married to Elliot and all the doubts that had constantly niggled her had returned. Why, had he married her, a woman ten years older than himself? Was he a man in love or an unscrupulous villain out for what he could get?

They had found out, a year ago, on her mother's death, and what they had discovered had been almost too awful to bear.

Part 2

Chapter One

2004

Going back 11 years

Elliot walked along the sea front at Cannes with Celia on his arm. They were a few days into their honeymoon. The place was bustling with activity and the harbour afloat with magnificent yachts. He studied the throng of boats, bobbing in their moorings that were owned by millionaires, wealthy aristocracy and businessmen.

That's me, before long, he thought, smiling at his new wife, eagerly anticipating being able to share in her large fortune. When they returned home he would make sure that he took control of it, whatever her bossy schoolteacher daughter said, and then live the life he'd always dreamed of. As for Celia, well he'd keep her sweet for as long as he could. After all without her there was no money or good lifestyle. She was presentable enough, for her age, well groomed, slim with a good dress sense, and he, himself, flaunting his new wardrobe of expensive clothes could easily pass for a rich entrepreneur on holiday. He felt in his prime and had finally achieved what he had been scheming for all his life, money-- and lots of it.

They had just lunched at an exclusive restaurant, eating caviar and drinking champagne not because he particularly liked it, but because he could, and now he sensed Celia's weariness. He'd send her for a rest and then he would be free to wander, view with envy and imagine which of these cruisers he would like to be master of.

"You're tired," he said. "Go and have a lie down. I'll just go a bit further and see what else is in the harbour. I'll be up later."

" I think I'll stretch out on the balcony and read my book," said Celia. "This heat takes some getting used to."

He saw her across the road then wandered on assessing each yacht as if he was a buyer at an exhibition. He stopped by a white, exquisitely sleek cruiser and watched an elderly man accept a cocktail from a white-coated attendant as he sat comfortably on deck, looking out to sea.

Mm-m -nice, he mused. *That's me before long.*

Elliot was like William, Celia's first husband in one respect and one respect only, --- they both craved money. However, the difference between them was simple. William had worked hard and honestly for his, whereas he, Elliot had taken a more devious road, befriending rich women and relieving them of a lot of their money under their very noses, whilst keeping their adoration and he'd been pretty good at it so far.

He didn't consider that he was breaking the law exactly. He was just helping himself to a slice of pie from those who had more than they needed. He had become a victim of circumstances at a young age, and he'd had to use his wits to get by. Because of this he'd lost any sense of guilt that he might have felt, a long time ago.

He had been born in the fifties into an aristocratic family. His father had inherited property and lived a life of luxurious idleness. Elliott and his brother, Douglas had found themselves growing up with their every need satisfied. Seldom had Elliot had to do anything that he didn't want to do until he went to public school. Being ordered about was not his cup of tea. He'd been a nightmare to his teachers, threatened with expulsion many times, but could be repentant also and managed to escape his father's wrath and behave, for some of the time anyway. His brother had been slightly easier to handle because he had considerable artistic talent and instead of kicking his heels, wondering what to do, spent his time creating his own *masterpieces.*

Elliot's father's wealth had been added to by that of his

wife, their mother, Isabella. She had been a beautiful debutante, only daughter of a knight and Elliot's father, Julian had fallen heavily for her beguiling charms.

However, after the two boys had left for public school she'd become a licentious handful and had eventually run off with a German Count who lived in a Schloss overlooking the Rhine. Her two sons had never seen her again. Their father had gone to pieces, lost his money on gambling and women and facing bankruptcy jumped off Clifton Suspension bridge to his death.

The two boys left in charge of an uncle, had soon broken away, when of age, accepting a generous allowance for five years. After that they had been on their own.

Douglas had scraped by, working in Art shops , galleries and eventually setting up on his own. They were close, he and Elliot, and, when needed would help each other out. Their desire for money was apparent. You can't grow up in opulence and not want an easy life and both boys had been quite prepared to cross the line to get it. They were essentially gentlemen, knew how to dress, speak eloquently and could easily mix with the elite of society.

So, whilst Douglas had persuaded young women to sit and be painted, Elliot had charmed them and been invited to stay at their expansive residences. Their generosity knew no bounds and he accepted all the gifts that were on offer with casual grace. He was taken to the races, the opera, attended balls and soirees and his good looks and eloquent manners enticed many young women to look upon him with favour. He did not offer marriage to any of them, after all he had nothing to give, so those that developed a *grande* passion for him were told, alas, that he was forced to leave them, temporarily, due to sudden commitments elsewhere. The promise to return was one that he never intended to keep.

He had developed an interest in cars, after all he'd driven in some of the best, Rolls Royces, Daimlers, Bentleys and had determined to own one himself one day.

When at home in Bristol, he'd befriended a man who owned a large garage full of exquisite motors. Elliot had shown great interest especially, of course in the most expensive ones and actually took a job there, worked hard and learnt all there was to know about cars, engines and mechanics so that when he had the money he could buy one and drive around, showing it off to all his aristocratic friends.

It had been early one summer evening when Elliot, driving along a quiet country lane to a rendezvous with his latest girlfriend, had witnessed an accident. A back tyre of the car in front of him had suddenly burst, causing it to zigzag on the road and crash into a tree. He had pulled up behind and dashed over to see if any one was hurt. The driver had obviously bumped his head and lay slumped across the wheel. A young woman was shaking him gently and screaming, "Dad, dad, are you alright?"

When Elliot had opened her door she'd turned, tearfully, to him and said desperately, "Oh, can you find a phone. My dad's hurt."

He'd found himself looking into the most beautiful face he'd ever seen. Sapphire eyes streamed with tears, delicate lips shook with worry, and her dark hair curled around her ears giving her whole face a charming elfin look. Elliot had been completely bowled over. He'd helped the young woman out, glanced at her father, who lay unconscious, sat her in his car and told her to wait while he ran along the road to find a phone at a house that he could see in the distance.

He'd looked at the damage to the car engine, whilst they waited for the ambulance. It would need a lot of work doing to it.

The young lady, Evelyn had climbed back in to be with her father who'd seemed to be showing signs of coming round.

"What shall I do about the car?" she'd said. "I don't know any garages. I'm just so worried about my dad. I can't think. I must go with him --need to contact my mum," and the tears had kept falling.

"I'll see to it," Elliot had said. "I work in a garage. I'll get it towed there and look it over. I'll let you know what the damage is. I just need to know how to contact you."

"That's easy," said Evelyn. We live at Orchard farm which is only a couple of miles up the road."

He'd written down the address and telephone number and then they'd heard the ambulance.

He too had been shaking as she'd departed with her father. He believed he'd met the girl of his dreams and he was not going to let her go.

Thankfully her father had not been seriously injured. His bump to the head had been superficial. He had, however, been left with a bad headache which tablets and a bit of rest should soon put right. He'd been very grateful to Elliot who had turned out to be the family's hero, not only being on hand when needed but also being able to organise and mend their Land Rover. He'd certainly got his foot in the door, was made very welcome and encouraged to visit thus enabling him to continue his romance with Evelyn.

He had been besotted with her and she with him. They'd married and moved into a cottage on the farm. Evelyn had been trained as an accountant and organised all the farm expenses, doing the books as well as managing many business accounts for other people. Elliot had used his knowledge to maintain all the farm vehicles and word had got round to other farmer's who sought his expertise also.

They had lived an insular life of adoration for each other and Elliot surprised himself by settling down and enjoying many years of honest work and normal living. Time had passed happily. Their son, Stephen, had been born two years later. He'd been their only child. His birth had been difficult for Evelyn and she was told that she probably would not conceive again. She had always been delicate. Many illnesses had taken their toll and when pneumonia had set in after a serious bout of 'flu she had not survived and Elliot, after ten years of marriage had found himself a widower, with a young son.

He had been absolutely heartbroken. The family battling their own misery, had, however, been a stalwart support to him, helping out with Stephen, stressing that they both would always have a home with them, trying to encourage him to carry on when really he'd just wanted to curl up and die.

He had started drifting away, going to stay with his brother for long periods of time. He'd left Stephen behind, looked after by his grandparents and the relationship between father and son had disintegrated as the years went by.

He'd felt guilty, of course, but he'd hurt, so badly. Time was no healer in his case. He knew that Stephen would be well looked after, be sent to a good school, but it wasn't until he reached eighteen that he'd plucked up courage and gone back to the farm to see him.

They were such good people, Evelyn's family, had not judged him, and he'd returned, like the prodigal son into their welcoming arms.

Stephen had been more difficult to win over, bore a huge grudge against his father because of his neglect, but had finally come around to tell him about his plans for the future, how he wanted to go to Agricultural College and try to get his own farm. His grandad had generously offered to help. Evelyn had older brothers who would inherit Orchard farm so he needed to be independent and make his own way. Elliot had gone away feeling very proud of him.

As for himself, he felt that now his son was grown up and had a purpose in life, he wasn't really needed, so reverted to character, set up a scam with his brother that could make them millionaires or, alternatively become locked up at Her Majesty's pleasure.

Chapter Two

Celia was glad to get out of the heat. She took the lift up to their luxurious penthouse apartment, poured herself a long cool drink, and kicking off her shoes padded out onto the balcony. She sighed as she settled on a lounger and sipped her drink. There was plenty of shade at this time of day, and being high up on the sixth floor she could see none of the hustle and bustle of the busy seafront nor hear any of the sounds that went with it. A slight breeze that was very welcome, ruffled the leaves of the potted palms that decorated the balcony and, finishing her drink, she lay back, absorbing the peace of the moment and pondering how greatly her life had changed since meeting Elliot.

She knew exactly what he would be doing now she had left him, wandering along eyeing all the wealth displayed in the magnificent yachts exhibited along the waterside. *Probably hoping to own one himself,* thought Celia, wryly. *No chance! They were all far too expensive, even the smaller ones.*

She was no fool, had got his measure, knew that the biggest attraction for him was her money. However she was certain that her family thought her gullible and had been taken in by his charms. There was no doubt that he was very presentable, tall, slim, with soft brown eyes and a cultured public school accent. To her he was always kind, considerate and loving. She could not fault him but, even in her happiest moments she knew that he was to be watched, that in all honesty he would not have wooed her, a woman ten years his senior, if she hadn't been able to give him the life of luxury for which she was sure he craved.

She would not believe that he was really selfish and bad. He had been so kind to her when Bonnie had died and had helped her a lot in those early years after William's death. She could easily have become a reclusive old lady, knitting, working for a charity, teaching piano to children, and becoming one of the elderly members of the community who met to drink tea and gossip, but he had lifted her spirits, taking on jobs that needed doing at the Manor, wining and dining her, going for long walks with herself and Mitzy and taking her on weekends away.

It was wonderful to have a companion again, to have someone to do things with. She would never forget William. He had been the love of her youth, but meeting Elliot and enjoying his companionship had been so welcome and she found herself invigorated every day by his energy and presence.

He had told her about his earlier life, the sad loss of his father and disappearance of his mother, how he hated school and the happiness he'd had with Evelyn. Celia knew that he had adored her, as she had loved William and how her early death had affected him so much that he'd sought comfort with his brother to escape the family that he had grown to love, -- and thus neglected his son.

She knew there were gaps in his life that he hadn't told her, especially where his brother was concerned. She had no idea how he'd lived or earned his living before he met her. Some things he never talked about, which was probably a good thing. What she didn't know was probably to her advantage, but it was wonderful that he'd made things better with his son Stephen, and when he introduced her to him and Lucille, his new daughter-in-law she felt that she'd gained a whole new family.

There had obviously been an estrangement between father and son and Elliot had come back into Stephen's life after he had finished at college and was settling in as one of her tenant farmers. Celia hadn't actually met the couple before. It was Barry who had dealt with the day to day running of the estate, but in Lucille Celia had found a very good friend and the introduction of the horses into her own stable yard, helping Lucille at the riding school, feeding and grooming the horses in her own back yard had given her a sense of purpose and encouragement for the future.

She had no idea how her life would progress or what

would happen between herself and Elliot. In fact she didn't really want to know. She was living the moment knowing that without him she would not be enjoying this wonderful holiday which, of course was their honeymoon. This could be the start of a very interesting time of her life and so long as he was with her they would be able to enjoy many more holidays together.

In all honesty, because of the age difference, she hadn't expected that he would ask her to marry him, or that she would even consider it, but when he did she had not the least doubt that entering into marriage with him was the right way forward even though she knew when he'd proposed, that he expected to outlive her and thus inherit Oakdene Manor.

So she was keeping him in the dark - hadn't told him, nor intended to, that there was no way this would happen. She wanted to prolong the happiness that he was giving her for as long as she could.

William had left Oakdene Manor to her with the understanding that it would then pass on to Anna, and on her death to Adam and there was nothing Elliot could do about it.

Once she'd agreed to marry him she had been to the solicitor and altered her will, leaving him a very generous allowance that she hoped would satisfy him. She wasn't that hard-hearted, but he was such an enigma that she really didn't know if she could trust him completely.

Many people might be curious as to why she had accepted him, believing that his interest in her lay in the property she owned, and not in her wifely qualities. However she was no fool, knew that if he was living with her, she would be able to monitor his day to day activities, and give him all the freedom and resources that he longed for as she tried to defer the moment that she dreaded when he would demand to visit her solicitor with the purpose of finding out and learning what was contained in her will and whether it would be in his favour.

If I were Elliot, Celia thought, *on returning home from*

our honeymoon, that's the first thing I would do.

Chapter Three

Their honeymoon was over and they were on the way back home. It had been a wonderfully relaxing time. They had enjoyed the Mediterranean climate, each other's company, meeting new people who appeared as well-off as themselves, living as the rich do and spending a lot of money, Celia's, of course.

Their days had been spent in comfortable luxury. Their penthouse suite was elegantly furnished and a special group of staff had been appointed to see to their every needs. Celia had made sure that Elliot had everything he desired especially money and a lot of freedom to do as he wished. Part of the day they spent together, walking along the seafront or meeting new acquaintances for a drink.

Occasionally Elliot had hired a car and driven her along the coast to see other places, east to Nice or west to Saint Tropez but in the afternoons Celia had been glad of a lengthy siesta, on their balcony to snooze or read and then Elliot would go out and about on his own, meeting his new-found friends and generally living the life that he had always craved for. He had been invited onto yachts, or for a game of golf and played the tables in the casino, losing and winning. Celia supposed that he was careful at how much he lost, especially as he felt that the money was now his own. So the time had passed far too quickly and both had enjoyed themselves, each in their own way.

Elliot had bought her a beautiful leather handbag paid for by a lucky win at the casino and now, on the homeward flight he kept dropping hints about how much he would like to own a *small* cruiser and spend his time sailing the warm Mediterranean Sea. Celia had kept quiet until she could stand it no longer.

"Forget about yachts," she'd said. "There's a surprise waiting for you at home."

"Really. What?"

"Ah, well, if I told you it wouldn't be a surprise."

With that he'd had to be content and, like a small boy, could hardly contain his excitement.

The surprise was standing in the drive when the taxi brought them home. The latest Aston Martin.

Elliot was thunderstruck, threw his arms about her, kissing her with blissful joy, then stopped and looked at her, his eyes filling up as he remembered his mission. Shame, for Elliot was not something that he had ever experienced but at this moment, facing a woman whose love and generosity towards him was boundless, he did, in all honesty, feel a twinge of sadness and almost disgust at his motives for cultivating her dependency on him.

So he took her for a ride, raced the country lanes, listened to her squeals as they tore round bends until finally returning home.

"I won't drive like that again," he said, laughing. "This car is far too valuable. I'm going to look after it, from now on." And he did. It was cleaned and polished, pampered and cosseted like a prize horse or precious trophy. He was also over the moon that he could visit Douglas in style and didn't have to use the little car that Celia popped around in, or the old estate Land Rover.

They settled down, happily at Oakdene Manor, Celia glad to have someone to share the burden of the house and estate, to cook for and look after. She was overjoyed that Elliot appeared to love his new position. He assessed every part of the land that they owned, walking about in stout boots, stick in hand, a deer stalker on his head in winter and always with his faithful new collie, Blake, by his side, replacement for Mitzy, who had recently died.

He noted every job that needed doing; fallen walls to be rebuilt, the stream to be unblocked in places, gates that needed repair and overgrown paths that needed clearing. To the tenant farmers he became a good friend as long as they maintained the standards that he required. All this he brought back to Celia, discussing, grumbling, always eager to show her how hard he was prepared to work. She supported him, backed him financially, knowing that he saw himself as owner of this large part of the Cotswold landscape.

The day was yet to come when he would realise that all of this would only last for as long as Celia lived. He had approached the family solicitor several times and been told, as approved by Celia, that he had nothing to worry about. What he chose to believe from that response was up to him. Celia did not go out of her way to discuss it.

He still visited his brother , but not as frequently, nor as often. He and Celia both spent time with Stephen and Lucille, Celia finding Stephen pleasant enough, but there was something about him that was disconcerting. She supposed it was because he was her tenant and thus felt that he wasn't her equal, but, in this day and age, in many respects this was an outdated notion.

Lucille, however, even though being much younger than Celia, was fast becoming a good friend. They went out together, shopping, visiting friends, to gymkhanas and shows and worked together building up a very popular riding school.

Anna, seeing and knowing that her mother was happy and content visited regularly but felt no real worries as she and James ploughed on with their own careers, Anna becoming a head teacher and James a heart consultant.

The years passed, it seemed, in peace and harmony but beneath the surface, there always niggled the question on both Celia's and Anna's minds, "Is this all too good to be true?"

Chapter Four

Elliot was not completely content. Something niggled him. He had acquired a beautiful home and a purposeful life in managing a large and profitable estate. Everything was going just as he had hoped and planned, or so it seemed, and yet his new wife still kept hold of the purse strings, very tightly. She continued to exclude him from knowing about and dealing with their finances and when he'd offered to take them over he was annoyed when Celia had said,

"It's alright, Elliot. I don't mind keeping my eye on things. It gives me something to do. You've no need to worry. If you need money just ask for it."

But this was not enough. All he wanted to know was how much money she had and to be able to have some control over how to spend it.

He decided to play snoop, so one day when she was out he searched her bureau but found little of interest in there. *There'll be a safe, somewhere*, he thought. *Now where is it?* He looked in the obvious places, inside cupboards and behind the larger pictures. He even went up into the attic and down into the cellar to search, but to no avail, so he returned to the study, which was the most likely place for it to be and eventually found it cleverly hidden behind the panelling in a corner of the room where he spotted a small button which, when pressed opened up a square panel to reveal it embedded in the wall. *Aha*, he thought, *found it*. Now for the combination? This was a real problem. There were six numbers needed. He tried a few ideas but it was an impossible task. He'd never be able to work it out, so feeling disgruntled he gave up.

But not for long. There was only one thing left to do. He would have to face Celia and question her. So the next day he looked her in the eye and asked, "Have you made a will, Celia?"

"There's always been a will, Elliot. It was made before

William died."

"So have you changed it now that we're married?"

Celia sighed. This was the question that she had been waiting for, and dreaded. She could not lie. She would have to tell him the truth.

"No, Elliot, I haven't. This house and estate was William's which he left to me during my lifetime and then to Anna and Adam."

"Oh!" His face said everything.

"But, you don't need to worry," she said. I will give you all you ask, if I can, whilst I'm alive and I've added a codicil that will give you a generous settlement if I die before you."

"Right," he said and walked away to strut the estate that would never be his in a fury that threatened to erupt like an active volcano.

Celia had known that he would not be satisfied with her answer and feared the outcome which was why she had kept the knowledge from him for as long as possible, and as the days progressed she sensed a change in him that she had expected but had wanted to postpone.

His enthusiasm for the estate dwindled. His trips to Bristol increased and sadly their happy, comfortable relationship began to crack.

Celia poured out her troubles to Lucille.

"I'm sorry for you," Lucille said. "I've never believed him to be the man that he appeared, and this attitude does not improve him in my eyes. I would take care, if I were you Celia. He is still very much an unknown quantity to us all and Celia was left with the distinct impression that Lucille and Stephen had no more knowledge of what Elliot was like, than she had herself.

However, after Elliot had been away for a good few weeks causing Celia to waken each morning feeling depressed and lonely, he suddenly returned full of energy and commitment, gave her a big hug, a large bunch of flowers, apologised for his reticent behaviour and hurried off to the estate office with a very excited Blake chasing after him, to catch up on what had been going on since he had left.

Suddenly the sun had come out and Celia was able to relax knowing that she had no longer to battle with estate business, although Lucille and occasionally Stephen had helped her, and that for some reason Elliot had overcome his gloom and appeared as happy as he had been before. She was not going to ask why, but would just enjoy floating on his enthusiasm and apparent care for her, whilst waiting to see what the outcome of his restored humour was all about.

She soon found out. He had obviously decided to spend her money while he could. He suggested that they get the decorators in to do the place up a bit. It was dowdy, in his opinion, the furniture ancient. Celia agreed - to a certain extent. The decorators came and painted walls and ceilings. New rugs and carpets were bought, a large TV replaced the old, smaller one and comfortable chairs were arranged suitably to view it. Upstairs bathrooms were refurbished and a new king-size bed bought for their bedroom. Elliot also fitted out a dressing room with a bed where he could sleep when he had bad nights, which he quite often did, apparently.

Celia realised that he needed his space. Theirs was a marriage of affection rather than of romance. They were not young lovers but two people for whom companionship was all important. Well, that is what she wanted to believe but knew in her heart that, for him, companionship was not enough. He was ruled by money and possessions and for that reason she was always wary of him.

She did agree, though, the house needed updating, but some of the oldest furniture, she insisted remained where it was. It belonged in this historic house. Not surprisingly Elliot agreed. He could see the value in it. The kitchen was also modernised with new cupboards and sink units and the utility room now housed a huge fridge/freezer. The old Aga remained. It still worked and Celia couldn't bear to part with it but it was supplemented by an electric hob and oven, so that the Aga could be shut down in the summer. Two old chairs still lounged beside it and the scrubbed wooden table remained, stretching across the middle of the room.

The progress of refurbishment took the best part of a year. As each room was transformed, things had to be moved and stored, precious items were wrapped carefully, this included, of course, photographs and paintings.

One day Elliot stood holding the painting of Oakdene Manor that he had just taken down from its position above the fireplace in the hall.

"You know, Celia," he said. "All these paintings look a bit drab and dirty. My brother is in the business, knows how to clean them and would do them all for a smaller fee than other professionals who offer the same service. Shall I take this one to him, first and let him prove what he can do?"

He was treading on dangerous ground and knew it. William's paintings were valuable both in monetary terms and sentimental ones. This one was probably the least in value but incredibly old, late seventeenth century, painted by Dunstable, whose landscapes were becoming more sought after as the years went by. It was of Oakdene Manor as it was then. Obviously it had changed over the years but was still easily recognisable from the painting. William had been over the moon when he'd found it. Not many people would be able to say that their house had been painted by a famous artist centuries ago.

This purchase had stimulated William's love of Art, the only hobby or leisure time activity that he had allowed himself, that of browsing round galleries and studios searching for an investment for his money. He had bought six altogether, knowing that their value would rise. He never told Celia how much they had cost, but she could imagine. Paintings sold for millions these days and the ones hanging in Oakdene were insured, but probably for nowhere near what they were worth. Thus to let Elliot take one to his brother to be cleaned was a consideration that she had to think long and hard about.

But allow it she did, hoping that she hadn't made a terrible mistake.

Elliot left a few days later with the painting but stayed only a short time in Bristol wanting to hurry back to start on his next big venture, improving the gardens and parkland. This included resurfacing the drive and paths, strengthening the bridge over the stream, cutting down some trees that had grown too large thus causing parts of the house to be constantly in shadow and replanting flower beds and the rose garden. His daily battle was with rabbits and moles. He worked alongside the villagers that grew vegetables in the walled garden, learning from them how to plant, nurture and protect vegetables and fruit from the predators that abounded there.

Celia was very impressed and happily paid all the bills that came in and was thrilled when he produced his first crops of, peas, carrots and potatoes as well as tomatoes, grown in a renovated greenhouse along one wall of the garden.

How she loved this purposeful new Elliot, whose eyes sparkled as he told her what he'd done and who seemed to relish her congratulations when he handed her a basket of produce cultivated by his own hand.

Yet she couldn't help the doubts and niggles that would not go away. Why was he doing all this when he knew that the house and estate would never be his? He must have a reason. Did she believe that he was just happy in his work- not really? He was embedding himself more and more deeply into her affections, every day, and for what reason? There could be only one. Any day she expected him to approach her again and mention the will in the hope of persuading her to change it in his favour.

Alas this was something that she would not do. Oakdene was her daughter's inheritance and Elliot was welcome to live and work here for as long as she, Celia lived, and afterwards he would still be looked after and could still be involved, but in her heart of hearts she knew that he would not settle for that. He wanted it all, the house, estate, money and prestige, now and forever.

However until that day came she was content and when he brought back the painting of Oakdene newly cleaned and looking wonderful in its old frame she was moved to tears and hugged him tightly as she gazed at its newly revealed splendour.

What she didn't see, above her head were her husband's eyes, steely blue, also focussing on the painting, whilst a slight sneer twisted his lips.

Chapter Five

2009

Celia and Elliot had been married for five years. Elliot's refurbishment of the house and gardens was complete, his running of the estate efficient and his rapport with the tenants harmonious. Celia could honestly say that she was pleased beyond all her wildest dreams with his consideration and care for herself and her property. She also enjoyed helping Lucille with the horses, housing two of them in her own stables, and pottered happily in her house and garden leaving all the heavy work to a twice weekly domestic help and a gardener/handy man who worked under Elliot's instructions.

She woke up every morning feeling relaxed and ready for the day, and went down to have breakfast with Elliot before he started his morning's work. Her happiness was undeniable, her health better than ever, but in the back of her mind a question always lingered. How long can this idyllic phase last and when if at all will the blissful bubble burst?

Three paintings had now been to Bristol to be cleaned. It was not a quick job and attention to detail was paramount.

"We wouldn't want any mistakes made," Elliot had said when excusing the length of time it took for each one to return and reminding Celia that his brother, Donald, had an Art studio to run as well.

Then, one day a knock came on the front door. Miriam, Celia's cleaner answered it and ushered into the lounge a tall, thin lady who looked a little familiar.

As Celia got to her feet the lady came towards her, holding out her hand.

"Hello, Celia, you probably don't remember me. I'm

Gwenda."

They shook hands, and then the penny dropped.

"Gwenda," said Celia, forcing a smile. " William's sister. I didn't recognise you. It's been a long time."

"I was at your wedding."

"Over thirty years ago! You probably don't know, then" said Celia, solemnly, "that William is dead. We did try to contact you but could only leave a message with yours and Harriet's previous neighbour."

"I did get the message but I was away travelling."

"Oh! --- but you could have contacted me, rung or sent a card. It was a very sad time for the family. I would have appreciated it."

"I thought about it, but decided to come personally instead."

"Nine years later!"

"Yes, well circumstances change, time passes."

In other words she hadn't cared enough, thought Celia.

It was hard to accept that this was just a spontaneous visit, being as she had seemingly disappeared from the face of the earth for a very long time. Gwenda had a reputation and most probably a reason for coming at this time, so as far as Celia was concerned she was going to treat her very warily indeed.

"So why have you come now?"

"I've been living abroad and decided to come home to see my daughter, Marcia. She wrote telling me of her father's death several years ago. Ron had been my first husband but he was no good and I divorced him. He was always having affairs but Marcia stayed with him. They seemed to rub along well enough together. She's married, now, but has no children. Her husband's in the Merchant Navy and away from home for long spells. She says she gets lonely and would love to see me. So I thought if we got on well enough I would move back to England and live near her. We need to get to know each other again. I'll also be near enough to visit you regularly. It's strange, as you get older how being part of a family seems so important."

"Indeed it does," said Celia, inwardly shuddering at the thought of having Gwenda on her doorstep. "Where does Marcia live?"

"Clevedon. It took me about an hour from her house to here. Marcia works as a solicitor's clerk and doesn't need her car during the week so I asked if I could borrow it so that I could visit you. I know I've a lot of bridges to build, but I hope you'll let me try."

"Ah, well, we'll see. Time's a great healer," said Celia, " and sometimes the past is best left behind us. Let's have a cup of tea." She led Gwenda into the kitchen and put the kettle on. She did not get out the best china but filled a couple of mugs with tea and placed them on the kitchen table with some plates and a tin containing a fruit cake.

"Do sit down, Gwenda," she said pointing to one of the modern kitchen chairs that they used every day when they sat at the table. Gwenda was well aware that anyone else would have been invited into the lounge for tea.

"So, are you still alone or have you remarried?" she asked, looking around the large, expensively equipped kitchen.

"Yes, Elliot and I were married five years ago. We're very happy. He's always busy as he's taken over running the estate. He'll be in shortly, I expect."

"How about you, Gwenda? Did you marry again or stay single," asked Celia?

"For a short while, yes. George was older. Looking for a companion really. I was quite happy to be that. He was a very kind and jolly man. We had a few good years until he died in a car accident. I missed him terribly. I found myself on my own, once again. He had four children, who inherited everything. He left me a few thousand and use of the house, but I was soon asked to go. I hadn't got on too well with George's family. They thought I was after his money and were pleased when I received very little from the will."

They saw through you too, thought Celia.

"So I took myself off to Spain, met a lovely little

Spaniard, Jose, and lived happily in his villa by the sea until last year when, sadly, he ate some dodgy shellfish and died. I was very upset. I didn't want to stay there without him, well I couldn't afford to. It seems he didn't own the villa, just rented it, so now I find myself on my own again and getting older, even a little sentimental, having this craving to see my family once more."

Celia wasn't taken in by this. It was obvious that Gwenda had sought out men with a bit of money but it hadn't done her any good. She was still penniless and homeless. *She's come here hoping for a hand-out*, she thought, *believing she has a right, as William's sister. If William had wanted her to have some he would have included her in his will -- but he didn't.*

Just at that moment the door opened and Elliot walked in. He was surprised to see a visitor.

"Elliot, this is Gwenda, William's younger sister. She's just dropped in, out of the blue, to visit us."

"Pleased to meet you," said Elliot, smiling his charm as he looked at her thin face, bird sharp eyes and angular body. She looked as if she had just visited a Charity shop, her long legs encased in unfashionable flares, and her flat-chested skinniness enveloped in a T shirt and stretchy cardigan.

She saw his critical glance and said, " I've had to do some hasty shopping. All my clothes are too light and thin for this climate. It's very hot in Spain at the moment."

Elliot helped himself to some tea, glancing as he did at Celia. As expected he could sense her tenseness. He'd heard about Gwenda, the black sheep, but hadn't expected her to turn up after all this time. There would be only one reason for her arrival. She was after some money. *There's obviously no man in her life any more,* he thought . *She could be dangerous now that she's getting older and looking like an old hag. Celia must realise that she's on the scrounge.*

"This is a lovely house," said Gwenda. "I knew William would do well for himself. He was always working."

Not like you, thought Celia. "Would you like me to show you around?"

"Oh, I'd love to," said Gwenda.

I'll bet you would, thought Elliot. Out loud he said. "I'll leave you to it, then, I promised to call in on Stephen. I'll see you later," and with that he escaped, not at all interested in Celia's in law from her first marriage. However he did recognise the greed that sparkled in Gwenda's eyes, and that worried him. He was very wary of her motives for reconciliation and hoped that Celia was too.

The house, now modernised, gleamed in its new comfortable splendour and as she showed her around Celia sensed that Gwenda was excitably impressed, especially with the paintings.

"I know a bit about Art," said Gwenda. "William was always dragging me round galleries. I can see he was an avid collector."

"Yes, and all the paintings are in the process of being cleaned by Elliot's brother. He has a gallery in Bristol, *Marshall's Art.*

"Mm, I'll have to go and find it, now I'm in the area," said Gwenda, and feeling that she'd had a good nose around and sensed the wealth that filled every corner of the house, she picked up her bag and announced that it was time to leave.

"I must go. Marcia will wonder where I've got to. It's been lovely seeing you, and your beautiful house. We must visit each other again, soon," and kissing Celia on both cheeks departed the house, climbed into a black VW and drove away.

A smell of insecurity seemed to hover in the air as Celia walked back into the kitchen. It felt like she'd had a visit from Cruella de Vil. Gwenda had been definitely snooping and the worry was in not knowing what she was going to do next.

Chapter Six

Elliot was worried. The visit of Gwenda, the witchlike, devious sister of his wife Celia's first husband, had caused an atmosphere. Celia had obviously been rattled and her contentment and happiness had taken a downward turn. He had assured her that he would not allow this horrible woman to wheedle her way into their settled family life. Her reasons for calling were obvious. They did not believe her to be the repentant, returning sister-in-law, and remained very wary of her, believing her motives to be demanding, scheming and totally intent on getting as much as she could of her brother's fortune.

Elliot liked to think that, even though he and Gwenda were after the same thing, Celia's money, that he was behaving in a much more humane fashion and basically did not wish any harm to come to Celia. He was certain that Gwenda had no scruples like that at all.

They were right. Their concern was justified. Gwenda became a limpet, a persistent presence in their lives. Every few weeks she returned, paying as she said a neighbourly visit to her sister-in-law. She would turn up without warning, even though Celia had suggested that she ring beforehand in case they were out. She would drop hints that she would love her own house but couldn't afford it, that living with Marcia was unsatisfactory because she was always at work. Then there was the problem of Marcia's husband, Tony, who had returned from sea and was, apparently, not pleased to find his mother-in-law installed as a permanent fixture.

Celia and Elliot listened and commiserated but were immune to her hinted hardship. If she had come out with it and asked for a loan it wouldn't have been so bad, but devious insinuations did not wash, especially as they occasionally found things missing, a silver jug from a cupboard, some cash left in a drawer and a necklace that Celia had taken off and put on a dish in the hall. How did

Gwenda manage it? They watched her like hawks all the time, but these items were gone and there was only one person who could have taken them. In fact Gwenda had taken the necklace but Elliot, realising this, decided to help frame her by taking the other things, himself.

On one visit she brought her daughter, Marcia. Double trouble, thought Celia, but in this instance she was wrong. In Marcia she discovered an ally. She was a very, confident young woman, did not look like Gwenda, thankfully. It was obvious that she knew exactly what her mother was after and, to be honest, admitted that she would be glad if she had her own house and was no longer under her roof. Whilst Gwenda was snoozing outside in a deckchair, Marcia opened up and told Celia a lot more about her.

"She was the mother from hell, Aunt Celia," she said, "and drove my father away. He was not the bad man that she said he was, but kind and sensitive. They must have loved each other to start with but, as I grew up the tension, arguments and hatred on her part forced him to dally with other women. I didn't blame him. I was a young teenager when she left. She hadn't wanted me, she certainly didn't want him, so she left with as much money as she could get and anything of value in the house. We didn't care. We were a lot happier without her. I liked living with dad. He worked in the council offices and encouraged me to stay at school and get good qualifications. When I married Tony, we moved to Clevedon but visited him often.

A few years ago mum sent a letter to us from Spain, with a photo of her lying by a pool. It was definitely meant to rub our noses in it, but she did include her address, knowing that I would let her know if anything happened to dad. When it did I wrote to her. It was the biggest mistake I've ever made. I wish now, that I hadn't, but I fell into her trap. She left Spain and came to find me and however much I long for it I know that she will not be going back again. She'll be the proverbial *thorn in the flesh* to both of us, and

I'm sorry that she's involved herself in your life."

"I'm so glad we're on the same side, Marcia," said Celia. "I must admit that Elliot and I are finding her visits annoying and a nuisance. Although she's a relative she's very difficult to like. I could do without her constant hints of poverty, but she's so thick-skinned and oozing niceness that she doesn't realise how distasteful she has become. I honestly don't know how to deal with her."

"She doesn't care whether she's liked or not, Aunt Celia," said Marcia. "Tony and I are trying to find her a place of her own. We've been looking at some flats in Clevedon, for her but she doesn't show much enthusiasm. I'm afraid she'd rather live with us at our expense. We'd probably have to help her with the rent as she says she has very little money, but I'd rather do that than have her permanently settled in our home."

"I know what you mean," said Celia. We could also find her a cottage on the estate, or give her rooms here but she would always be around, under our feet and I don't think Elliot and I could bear it. We believe she's already helped herself to some money and jewellery."

"Oh, no," said Marcia. "She said she'd won some money at Bingo and was able to buy a new dress. I'm so sorry, Aunt Celia, will you let me repay you."

"No, no, of course not, but watch out for anything that you have yourself, that could be valuable. She's like a ferret down a rabbit hole."

"Don't worry, I will."

The visit ended. Celia felt that she had found a friend in Marcia, even though Elliot wasn't too sure.

"Someone with a mother like Gwenda can't help but have inherited some of her characteristic traits," he said snidely. *Secretly he didn't want anyone else influencing or befriending Celia.*

The situation did not improve and Celia's health began to suffer. She would wake up with a headache that she couldn't shift until later in the day when she'd dosed herself with tablets. She was constantly tired and her appetite dwindled. Elliot became concerned.

"You ought to see a doctor," he said. "You're worrying all the time about Gwenda's next visit, and it's making you ill. The next time she comes I'm sending her away."

The climax came, one morning, when Celia was lying on a couch in the darkened lounge. She had nodded off but woke when she heard the phone. Knowing that she was alone in the house she put her feet to the floor, preparing to stand up but suddenly her head went dizzy, her legs gave way and she fell down spread-eagled on the carpet. A few moments passed and she tried to get up but she could only move her left arm and leg. All her right side and part of her face was completely numb.

I've had a stroke, she thought. She was terrified, knew that she'd have to stay lying on the floor until Elliot found her. The phone was in the hall, she'd never be able to reach it.

Fortunately Elliot, who had been working in the Estate office crossed the yard to the house to check on her. She'd been particularly bad that morning and he hadn't been able to concentrate. He did not want her to die just yet. She was worth too much to him. As he walked into the kitchen he called, "Celia, where are you?" but he was met with silence. Then he heard a trembling murmur.

He rushed through the hall and into the lounge and there he found her, lying on the floor.

"Celia, - Celia. What's happened?" But she could not answer him. She just stared with pleading eyes. He grabbed a cushion and put it gently under her head, covered her with a blanket and dashed to the phone. Never in his life had he been so frightened and felt so helpless.

He held her hand until the ambulance came and sat with her as they travelled to hospital. He rang Anna and Lucille from the waiting room, and was very relieved when the doctor finally came and confirmed that the stroke was not as serious as they had first supposed. Already some feeling was returning to Celia's side but it was too early to say whether she would walk again. They were going to move her to a ward and he could go and sit with her.

Tears watered his eyes as he saw her sitting propped up in bed.

"Elliot," she murmured, with half a smile. "I'll be alright. Don't worry."

His emotion touched her heart. She believed he did care, just a bit.

"They say your movement will improve," he said, "but not immediately. You musn't worry. I'll do everything I can to look after you" - and he actually meant it.

It wasn't long before Anna and James came, Anna in a flush of worry at seeing her mum so helpless.

"Oh mum," she cried hugging her gently."What happened?"

Elliot told them, aggressively blaming Gwenda.

"That woman has caused nothing but trouble ever since she first knocked on the door - all the aggro, insinuations, pleading poverty. It's the worry of it that has caused your mum's stroke. I never want to see her miserable face again."

"Hush, Elliot," muttered Celia softly.

Anna, who hadn't actually met Gwenda found this hard to understand, but from phone calls with her mother over the last few months she'd realised that Gwenda's invasion into their lives was causing them a lot of anxiety.

"Well, let's forget Gwenda and concentrate on you first, mum, getting you well enough to come home. I'll apply for some leave and come and help Elliot. If Gwenda turns up she'll have us both to contend with. I've never met her. Dad despised her. There's obviously little good to salvage in her character but her visits to Oakdene must stop. Marcia shouldn't let her use the car so much. I'm a bit suspicious of her intentions, actually.

With Anna as an obvious ally Elliot left her and James with Celia to go home and bring back a few essentials. His cage had been rattled but perhaps the scenario wouldn't be too bad. Celia was alive. He was the hero and Gwenda definitely the villain . Just as it should be, he thought with a smile.

Anna visited her mother regularly in hospital. She was there for many weeks as the staff monitored her progress and tried to get her mobile. However age was against her and it became clear that she would not walk again nor have much use in her left arm.

Anna realised that she would have to work with Elliot to ensure her mother's future care. They didn't want to put her in a home. She knew that she and James would have to trust him, after all she'd seen how happy her mother had been since she'd met him and how their marriage of five years appeared to be settled and content.

Oakdene Manor would need a lift for a wheel chair and some alterations such as a sit in shower and rails in Celia's bathroom, before she could go home.

Anna had no choice, and James reluctantly agreed that Elliot should be given Power of Attorney as well as herself. At this moment she did not live near enough to make more than weekend visits. She could not give up her job as a head teacher without several months notice, but she might have to consider this if relying on Elliot proved unsatisfactory. So she had to leave him in charge and he would need to be able to withdraw money when he needed it. Celia's monthly income came from the interest of multiple accounts that was paid into her bank account. Elliot would be able to draw on this to cover expenses.

A salary would be needed also for a live-in nurse, so that Elliot could continue with the Estate business .

Finally Celia came home, rode up to her bedroom in the new lift and met Helen, her nurse. Helen was a strong, energetic young woman, trained in geriatric care and was prepared to do anything required, even cook, on the days that Miriam the cleaner did not come in.

So Elliot, with his house well organised by efficient

women, was able to carry on much as before, running the estate, visiting his brother and his son, and best of all having, at last, his fingers on Celia's money.

Part 3

Chapter One

2012

3 years later

Stephen had been farming Beeches farm on the Oakdene estate for ten years. His initial delight in having his own farm, even though it was a tenancy, was at an all time low. He hadn't made it pay and he was up to his ears in debt.

It had all started so well with his grandad's encouragement and generous gift of money, his loan from the estate to buy machinery and equipment and his initial harvest of wheat, barley and oil seed rape.

During that first year he had married Lucille who he'd met whilst he'd been studying environmental studies at University. She had been doing Business Management. When she moved in she had done her best to make the old farm house comfortable and homely even though they'd little money for furniture. She had scrounged anything she could from her parents home. They'd much more than they needed both in furniture and in money. That was Stephen's opinion anyway. She'd searched junk shops and charity outlets and also bought some things on credit so, as long as they made the payments they had a reasonably furnished house to live in.

Lucille's main interest was horses. Her father had been a jockey but now was manager of a racing stables. She'd grown up around valuable horses, exercising, grooming and feeding them and was desperate to run her own stables and teach youngsters how to ride.

Stephen was keen to encourage her and had borrowed more money to convert an old building on the other side of the farmyard into stables. When these were complete Lucille's father acquired some ponies for her, and her business began. But their expenses were mounting up.

Then Elliot, Stephen's father, who, now that they were no longer estranged, often came to stay and help, met Celia, the owner of Oakdene Manor and estate of which Stephen's farm was one of the tenancies. They had become friends when Bonnie, Celia's little dog had died as they were walking through the village. His father had been first on the scene and an immediate hero with Celia. Their friendship had blossomed into marriage and his father had become manager of a vast estate and married to a woman who, it was said was worth -- a fortune.

It had all seemed above board. Stephen did not know his father well enough to have any suspicions and the advantages to himself and Lucille were bound to be beneficial, with his father's support and backing.

When Lucille had met Celia for the first time, she'd found her very easy to get on with. They had gradually built up a rapport, even though they were a generation apart, and had become good friends. Through this relationship Lucille had been able to interest Celia in her riding school, telling her how she wanted to expand the business and wondering if Celia would like to become involved. She had spotted the derelict stables at Oakdene Manor and seen the possibility of Celia housing and looking after a few horses there. By using the stables at Oakdene and thus involving her she'd hoped to expand the business especially if Celia was happy to donate money towards it.

There appeared to be no ulterior motive on Lucille's part although Elliot may possibly have had something to do with suggesting it. However Celia had taken to Lucille straight away and admired her ambition, and from that point of view she was prepared to help with money and the use of her stables. in fact looking after the horses was an added incentive for her to get up and be busy every morning.

For a few years everything had gone well. The stables had made money and they'd kept their heads above water.

The riding school had proved very popular, but that had all changed when Gwenda came on the scene and Celia had had her stroke, which meant that she could no longer help Lucille.

It hadn't been easy for Stephen either, having his father going from helping his tenant son to becoming the husband of his employer and thus living the life of Lord of the Manor. He had spent his childhood years resenting his father's neglect. He'd been only eight when his mother had died. He could remember her fair hair and blue eyes, that he himself had inherited. Also her love for him and the happiness they'd had as a family. He'd realised that his father had suffered greatly by her death, but couldn't understand why he'd left, without him.

"He's still got me," he'd sobbed in his grandma's arms. "Why didn't he take me with him?" She could only comfort him, for she had no answer to his distress. However they had been wonderful. No grandparents could have done more. Also there were his uncles and cousins all eager and willing to do all they could for him. He knew he was loved, had a home, and a family but this had been forever overshadowed by the neglect of the one person who didn't seem to care. Occasional visits were few and far between. Each time there had been tension on his behalf. He had not welcomed his father, and this stopped Elliot from visiting altogether.

Never once did his grandparents criticise his father in front of Stephen. They had lost Evelyn, Stephen's mother, too, and their pain was always with them.

So Stephen had grown up with his father having become a stranger to him, until the day that he reached twenty one when he had turned up in a Land Rover and handed him the keys.

"It's not new, but only a couple of years old ," he'd said. "I've checked it all over. It's in perfect condition. I hope it will be useful to you, now that you are twenty one. Happy birthday, son."

Stephen had been dumbstruck. Was this a peace

offering, an apology for his neglect? Should he accept it? He'd looked at his grandparents who'd also appeared stunned, but then his Grandma had rushed forward and put her arms around his dad saying, "Oh, Elliot, how generous. Come in, we'll have some champagne."

His Grandma had known just how to cope with the situation and before long they were all seated and feeling more relaxed. Stephen had shaken his father's hand and thanked him, but his father had pulled him into a hug, whispering, "I'm sorry, lad. I've neglected you so badly. It's time to make amends."

Now that Stephen had his own farm Elliot had visited him in his new situation many times, staying for several weeks at a time and helping on the farm. Stephen was only able to employ casual labour and his father's assistance was greatly appreciated. However he was still an enigma to him.

"Where do you live then, dad?" he'd asked one day.

"I stay with Douglas, my brother. He's got a house near his Art Gallery."

"He isn't married, then?"

"No, he was once, but it didn't work out. We get on well together. He was a great support to me after your mother died."

"But how do you make a living? Land Rovers are expensive to buy? "

"Oh, I get by," Elliot had said, tapping his nose and winking. This had made Stephen even more curious about what his dad got up to.

He'd talked it over with Lucille."Here we are, struggling to make a living and yet my father has now not only married a wealthy widow but seems to have some other means of making money as well."

"I think it's all to do with his brother," said Lucille. "They are so close, could be a couple of villains for all we know. He didn't come to our wedding but he did to your dad's. It's almost as if he only shows his face when it might be worth his while."

"I'm surprised, though, that it's always dad who goes to Bristol," said Stephen. "If I hadn't met Uncle Douglas that time I could almost have imagined that he didn't exist. It all adds to the mystery of what they get up to when they're together in Bristol."

"All I know is," said Lucille that Celia has been a good friend to me and now that she's so debilitated from a stroke I'm going to keep a keen eye on your father and make sure that he doesn't cause her any more distress."

Chapter Two

2010

Two years earlier

Gwenda knew that her visits to Oakdene Manor were unwelcome but she also knew that they were not going to stop. She had never felt the presence of money more than when she sank into a luxurious chair in the expensively furnished lounge and looked at the valuable items all around her, from porcelain to paintings. Her brother, William had done well for himself, and she intended to have a share of his wealth, especially since that pseudo toy boy had come on the scene, obviously on the scrounge, and persuaded Celia to marry him.

However her wiles had not paid off. Even taking Marcia with her, on one occasion, who seemed to immediately get on with Celia, hadn't made any difference. They had offered her nothing, in fact, they seemed to find her presence annoying, even though she put on her pleasantest face and most amiable manner. They must have found out something about her, probably from Marcia, --- miserable tell-tale. Either that or Elliot was bad-mouthing her to Celia. Gwenda recognised a gold digger when she saw one and knew that he would do all he could to stop her from getting so much as a penny. Also Celia, lately had even pretended to be ill when she called, and Elliot had completely avoided her.

Well, she'd succeed one way or another even if it was just helping herself to the odd little knick knack or piece of jewellery that might be lying about.

Today, however, she had decided to follow another lead and discover a bit more about the Marshall brothers. Celia had mentioned that Elliot's brother, Douglas, owned an Art Gallery in Bristol and was in the process of cleaning some of the paintings that William had bought and hung in Oakdene Manor.

Leaving Marcia's house one morning she made her way to the address that she had looked up and was pleased to find that *Marshall's Arts* was in a salubrious part of town, and breathed Victorian elegance. It was a large stone building set back from the road with big windows and a sweeping drive leading to some parking bays to the one side. An artistic sign near to the road announced its existence.

Mm, she thought. *No penny pinching here* as she walked towards the entrance where a flunkey, smartly suited stood, ready to open the door. He was tall and beefy looking. *A heavy,* thought Gwenda. There must be some value inside and, tingling with anticipation she moved forward through the door.

She nodded, condescendingly, to the big man as she walked in and gazed around at the spacious entrance hall and the many rooms that led from it.

Two, ladies sat behind a desk, eyes on computers, but one immediately stood and greeted her with a smile. "Good morning, madam," she said. "May I be of assistance?" *Very upper class,* thought Gwenda - *well, my dear, just listen to this* and she started to speak in stilted English with a few Spanish words thrown in. After all she'd lived in Spain long enough.

The woman was all over her, pointing out the different rooms, giving her a catalogue, treating her as a foreign aristocrat. *It's a good job I dressed up a bit this morning,* thought Gwenda, as she stroked her second hand coney fur coat and exposed a diamond necklace that belonged to Celia but had somehow got into her pocket.

Gwenda strolled around, studying the paintings. She had little knowledge about art and wasn't really interested but lingered as if she were. A few names seemed familiar and many were priced- very expensively in the catalogue, prices she wouldn't pay even if she could afford to.

Suddenly she spotted one that immediately caught her attention. If she wasn't mistaken she was looking at Oakdene Manor, as it must have appeared several centuries ago. *Now then, I've seen that one before*, she thought. She looked at the price in the catalogue. *Wow! It's never worth that much.*

"I presume this is an original," she said to the assistant.

"Oh yes, madam. It's by John Dunstable. Mr. Marshall hung it there some months ago, after he'd spent a long time cleaning it."

"It looks very familiar, just like an old house that I passed by last week," said Gwenda. "I think it was called Over-- no Oken - Oakenh--- manor ---"

"You mean Oakdene Manor," said the assistant. "That is the subject of this painting. Fancy you recognising the house especially as it must have changed over the centuries. This is a very old painting. What a coincidence."

Indeed, thought Gwenda. *There's no coincidence about it. One painting in this gallery and the same one in Celia's house and if this is the original what does it make the other? So that's your game, is it, Douglas and Elliot Marshall,--- forgery? What a money spinner!*

She was jubilant, but didn't show it. Instead she thanked the assistant, gracefully, leaving the impression that she would soon return in order to buy some paintings for her new house, and left the building, casually strolling, nose in the air up to the flunkey demanding that he flag her down a taxi. She thanked him, condescendingly as he held the door open for her and settled back as it drove away. When she was out of sight of the gallery she told the driver to stop and got out, paid him, reluctantly and caught a bus to the station. She hadn't money to burn, not yet, but, just you wait, Elliot Marshall, for I'm going to demand a very large piece of your artistic pie.

It was later that evening that Marcia answered the phone. She then hurried into the lounge where Gwenda was sitting watching the News, or pretending to, whilst plotting her next move.

"That was Elliot," she said, with a sob in her throat. "Celia's had a stroke and is in hospital. He thinks you should postpone any future visits until they know what her recovery is likely to be. How dreadful, poor Celia. I've only met her once but she seemed such a lovely lady," said Marcia.

She looked at her mother when she didn't answer. She was actually smiling and there was a brightness in her eyes.

"So, a stroke. She'll not recover from that," Gwenda remarked.

Marcia couldn't believe her callous attitude.

"Really, mum. Your sympathy astounds me," she said sarcastically, and left the room. Her mother was completely lacking in compassion and seemed almost pleased at the news. *She probably is,* thought Marcia, *and hoping that there might be something in it for her.*

Gwenda sat, thinking. This changed things, hopefully for the better. Celia would probably have a lengthy stay in hospital, maybe permanently. She would probably not improve much, and Oakdene Manor would be left to Elliot or at least in his charge. *Not likely*, she thought. It could be hers if she played her cards right. She could go to the house and challenge Elliot for possession, but she didn't want Marcia to know. If she managed to blackmail Elliot successfully she was not sharing it with her.

Over the next few days she worked out her strategy. She had knowledge that could make her fortune. Elliot hadn't a leg to stand on. If he didn't want Anna and James to know about his artistic fraud he would have to leave. Then she would be able to put on her caring face and turn into an indispensible aunt who would then be invited to live out her days in luxury at Oakdene Manor, as Anna's aged relative.

On the day that she chose to carry out her plan she waited

until Marcia had gone to work, wrote her a letter, thanking her for her hospitality and saying that she wished Celia well, but that she had decided to go back to Spain as she missed the warmth, and her friends. *I'll keep in touch*, she said.

But Spain was not her destination. Instead she made her way to Oakdene Manor intending to force Elliot to give her some money and let her move in. She was sure that she could make herself very comfortable and there was nothing that he could do about it.

Chapter Three

2010

A week later

Elliot should have been on cloud nine, but for some reason he wasn't.

He was sitting, alone, in the kitchen at Oakdene Manor, sipping some soup and half watching the news on the small TV that stood on the dresser. It was a week since Celia had had her stroke. He had been to see her that afternoon, held her cup and chattered idly as she dribbled her tea. He hated to see her like this. The doctors and nurses hadn't told him or Anna much about what recovery she would make, if any, but he knew that this stroke would change all their lives, and he wanted to make sure that it was to his advantage. He hoped that Anna would be so wrapped up in worrying about her mother that she would just allow him to carry on as he had been doing.

Thus he would have Oakdene Manor to himself. He knew all about the estate, had been running it superbly-- his way. He would, if Celia died, have been able to settle very happily as inheritor, but in this instance he had been thwarted as William, Celia's first husband had made sure that everything went initially to her and then to their daughter Anna, who, backed by her interfering husband, James, would own everything. As for himself he was supposed to exist, somehow, on an annual allowance. He was not prepared to accept that.

However in the last week events had changed to his benefit. Anna had relented and agreed to give him joint Power of Attorney. She was too concerned about her mother to stop and think whether she should put her trust in him, but he had managed to instil in her the fact that he was in earnest about helping, due to his worry and love for

Celia. Because of this he had virtually won her over and rubbed his hands with glee at the thought of finally being able to have some control over his wife's money.

In his own weird way he had to admit that he missed Celia. She was a loving presence, very easy to get on with and he wanted her home, even if she was unable to do things for herself. They could still have some years together and he would be able to carry on in the roll that he thrived on. The years since their marriage had been happy. He'd welcomed Celia's involvement with Lucille and the horses, and the building of bridges with Stephen had been comfortably rewarding.

But then a dark cloud had appeared on the horizon with the arrival of Gwenda, William's sister. They both knew that she was a conniving woman, the black sheep of the family. No amount of smiles and pleasantness had fooled them. Celia had been told, by William that she had always been difficult and selfish and her arrival and constant visits were proving him to be right. Gwenda was trouble and the only reason she had turned up in their lives was because she wanted and thought she deserved to have some of her brother's money. Elliot was sure that the knowledge of what she was after had seriously upset Celia and he was certain that this had contributed to her stroke.

As he sat there, deep in thought a knock came on the back door. When he opened it he found the subject of his thoughts, Gwenda standing purposefully on the step, bag in hand. He immediately tried to close the door but the wretched woman put her foot in the way.

"Good evening, Elliot," she said, pushing her way in."That's not very hospitable of you."

"What do you want? I'm not in a good place at the moment," he said, looking miserable and downcast. " I rang and told your daughter that my wife, Celia has had a stroke and is in hospital. I'm really worried about her. She's very ill and may not be able to walk again."

"I know that and can see that you're very upset," said Gwenda sarcastically.

"Very fortunate for my purpose."

Elliot looked at her, suspiciously, wondering what she meant.

"Aren't you going to ask me why I've come?"

"No, why should I?"

"Because, I know something about you that would damn you in the eyes of the world."

Elliot began to feel sick. "You're talking rubbish, you silly woman."

Gwenda bristled. The knives were out.

"I've come to stay for a few days. I'll tell you why in a minute after I've carried my things through into the hall."

"Oh, no you won't. You're not welcome. I know your game. You're on the cadge for anything you can steal. We know you've taken things from here before."

Gwenda grinned. "So why didn't you hand me over to the Police? It wouldn't be because they might find out something about you, would it?" She then pushed past him into the hall, with her bag. She set it down near the stairs and looked around. She saw magnificence in the wide oak staircase and the carved stone fireplace, centrally placed, but a gleam of absolute victory sparkled in her eyes as she saw what hung above it.

"What a lovely painting, by the way. It looks good up there above the fire,

--- and even better in Marshall's Art gallery where it's worth a lot of money if it sells. What's the value of this one, I wonder?"

Elliot was struck dumb. This was beginning to feel like his worst nightmare.

"I don't know what you're talking about," he bluffed.

"Oh, I think you do," Gwenda replied. "Forgery, theft --- "

They looked at each other. Hatred in his eyes, triumph in hers.

He saw trouble ahead for himself and Douglas. How had this fiendish woman found out about their painting scam? They had done so well, over the years. Nobody that they had dealt with had been suspicious or imagined that they were dishonest until now with the arrival of this double-crossing relation of Celia's. Douglas had been a success with his Art Gallery. It exuded style and class that had been a good frontage for the other way they made their money.

"What do you want?" he asked gruffly.

He knew, of course.

She mentioned a sum.

"Are you mad? I can't find that sort of money."

"I think you can. I'll just stay in this house until you give it to me."

"What! Never! You can get out right away," and moved forward to grab her and physically manhandle her through the door.

She stepped back, putting her hand up to stop him.

"I don't think so. I'll only come back, again and again. You'll never get rid of me unless you pay me."

They looked each other in the eyes. Elliot could see her resolve, but she was just a woman taking her chance with a man who had been a schemer all his life. *Time to soft soap the old bat,* he thought.

"Alright," he pretended to back down. "I'll get you some money, but It'll take time. Give me to the end of the week."

He had, as yet, no money to give her, but she didn't realise that. She believed that he feared *the hand of the law* coming down on him if he didn't keep his word. Knew that she would go straight to the Police if he didn't come up with the money.

"You can't stay here. I don't trust you and people might talk," he sneered. I'll pay for you to stay a few nights in a hotel. Come back on Friday."

She didn't argue because she knew he hadn't a hope in hell of wriggling out of this one, and decided that a trip to Weston-Super-Mare would be very enjoyable, at his expense.

He was generous, surprisingly, and also offered to drive

her to the station, after which he sat in deep thought--- but not about how to get the money.

There was no alternative. He hadn't wanted it to come to this but he had no choice. His whole livelihood was in the hands of a conniving, threatening woman and she had to be stopped.

On the Friday morning he rang and asked her to call later in the day. It would have to be after 7pm as he had other commitments and couldn't make it any earlier,-- *Not exactly true. He needed her to come at night when it was dark.*

" --- but you can stay the night and leave the next day."

Gwenda was overjoyed. Things were going her way. Elliot had conceded, was going to give her a huge amount of money and allow her to stay the night. What he didn't know was that she intended to stay at Oakdene Manor forever, --- and what she didn't know was that he had planned for that.

She travelled by train and then bus arriving at almost the right time. When she knocked on the back door there was no answer so she tried the handle and found it was unlocked. The light was on in the kitchen and so, without any scruples, she went inside calling, "Elliot! Elliot!" Her heart began to thump loudly. *Was this the moment when her life would change?*

She heard no movement, no answer from him so she looked around. Where was he? Her hands suddenly went clammy and her face paled. She feared that something was wrong. Then she spotted a note on the table.

It said, briefly, "Come across to the office."

Of course that's where he would be. She relaxed a little and stepped outside crossing the courtyard towards a light that shone from one of the office windows.

She did not knock but opened the door and walked in.

He was there, facing her.

"Good evening, Gwenda," he said, and before she could reply, lifted up his hand. In it was a pistol pointing straight at her head.

She gasped, prepared to run but the thud from the silenced gun pierced her forehead and rested in her skull. She fell, lifeless, to the floor. Greed for money had decided her fate.

He dragged her outside to the hole that he had prepared, threw in the gun and then her body and buried her as he had planned.

Chapter Four

2010-2013

Over the next year Celia seemed to improve. She was so glad to be home and very appreciative of all that Elliot had done for her comfort and welfare. He had installed a lift, made alterations to the ensuite bathroom and hired a nurse Helen to look after her. Helen was a strong Cornish girl who turned out to be extremely capable and very willing to do anything.

All this had been and was costly but pleased Anna greatly when she visited and saw the efficient household that Elliot had created for her mother. Celia would wake up and have her breakfast brought to her on a tray, then Helen would help her shower and dress. They would go down in the lift and Helen would wheel her to wherever she wanted to be. She had a day bed by the window in the lounge and a moveable table on which drinks were placed, and her Laptop computor. Elliot was teaching her how to use it and, even with one hand she could surf the web or contact her friends.

The doctor came regularly and a physiotherapist, who worked her wasted limbs. Lucille and many friends came to visit, talking to her and encouraging her to speak and use her hand.

Lucille often took her to see the horses at her stables. Elliot had bought a special car fitted with a ramp that would enable Celia to be lifted in and out whilst sitting in her wheelchair. She loved these outings and sat, happily at Lucille's stables watching the children learning to ride. She knew all the horses and enjoyed feeding and stroking them.

Elliot took her on short trips in the car, to Cheltenham, pushing her along the Promenade and through the Long Gardens lined with elm and horse chestnut trees, or to sit by the river and feed the ducks and have a cup of tea. Once or twice he took her to the races, but she eventually let him go on his own as she found it too exhausting. *He'll probably enjoy it better without me, anyway*, she thought, and she never asked how much money he won or lost, nor did he tell her.

Other trips, if the weather was nice were to Bourton-on-the-Water where the river meandered down through the centre of the village, Broadway and Stow-on-the -Wold. They always had a happy time on all these visits and Elliot found himself, surprisingly content when he realised how much enjoyment he was giving her. He seemed a man transformed and Celia revelled in his care and thoughtfulness.

In the evening they would watch TV or ask friends round. Helen was a good cook and didn't mind preparing food for them.

Elliot's motives, known only to himself were mainly to keep Celia alive for as long as possible, and she was happy to believe that he was concerned and cared for her. In all honesty she was the only person he was bothered about. As he planned his next moves even Stephen, his son, was not his major concern. Every thought, action and planning in his life revolved about acquiring Celia's money. So long as she was alive he had his hands on it, but what happened to it after her death when Anna inherited instead of him, was his main concern.

However, it was confirmed eventually, that Celia would most likely not walk again. The slight improvement in that first year reached a plateau and, it was accepted by everybody, sadly, that this was it. Celia knew and coped well. Sometimes a few tears were wiped away by Helen, when she tried to do something, but couldn't.

One thing that always made her happy was the little stray cat that had appeared on their doorstep and would sit on Celia's knee. It was black but had patches of white and she loved it. She would stroke its soft fur, listen to it purr and wonder where it had come from.

"It's a mystery," said Helen, knowing full well that Lucille's cat had had kittens recently, and that she had chosen this one especially for Celia.

Elliot, meanwhile continued to run the estate very efficiently. He needed to. Anna visited every weekend and she seemed very satisfied with the way he was dealing with everything. Every bit of money that came in and went out of the accounts was recorded and James kept a regular check on all the figures. Elliot was quite happy with this scrutiny. He knew that the ball was in his court and he could fill his pockets and disappear whenever he wanted to, which knowing the murderous deed that he had been forced into, could be at any moment.

Anna was far more concerned with her mother's health rather than her finances as she seemed to be getting weaker every time she visited.

Celia's second stroke occurred just after Christmas of the second year. Anna, James and Adam had come to stay and Lucille had helped Anna prepare the Christmas dinner. Helen had been given a well-earned holiday, so a happy family gathering, including Stephen and Elliot, of course, sat around the table.

Celia loved it, knew there wouldn't be many more for her, and spent her time listening and watching, as presents were unwrapped, crackers pulled and games played.

It was a few days later that they found her, slumped in her chair, her face contorted. It was obvious that another stroke had caused this. She was taken to hospital and rallied a little but everybody knew that probably this time she would not return home. She was more helpless, less coherent and lay in bed clutching Anna's hand and looking at Elliot with tearful eyes.

Her case was discussed with the nursing staff who felt that a home where she could be cared for permanently would be better for her. It was very distressing but Anna asked Elliot if she could choose one that was close enough for her to visit every day. She chose *The Cedars* which was just outside Bristol. She was worried that Elliot would be upset at the distance he would be from her but he went along with it quite readily. He would still see Celia regularly, combining a visit to her with one to his brother. However he now had bigger fish to fry. Keeping Anna away from Oakdene was a necessity, so, with her mother now being in Bristol there was little need for her to drive up to see if all was well, which played nicely into Elliot's hands. He would still be in charge of the house and estate and thus would have the freedom to do exactly what he had always planned.

So as Celia had gone, never to return, Elliot sold the big car. It was no longer needed, and paid off a tearful Helen on her return from holiday. After that he let it be known that he had virtually closed the house down. He used only the office in the yard, and the kitchen, occasionally his bedroom. Most evenings he spent with Stephen and Lucille and he visited Celia twice a week when he went down to Bristol to stay with his brother.

Knowing of Stephen's disillusionment due to his lack of making money he encouraged him to use his land differently by turning a field into a caravan park. He paid for some builders to construct shower rooms and toilets and it wasn't long before the site became very popular. The Cotswolds were an attractive holiday place for many people. It also benefited Lucille's riding school and the addition of a small animal farm for children that housed animals such as a donkey, geese, rabbits and guinea pigs brought many visitors who paid to come in, feed and stroke them. Stephen also sub let his other fields. He could do anything now that his father was in charge, and was becoming more and more indispensible to Elliot who encouraged him to take over much of the running of the estate.

This was a deliberate ploy by Elliot, because, unbeknown to Stephen, he was preparing to put all his plans in motion ready to make a quick exit when Celia eventually died.

Chapter Five

2013

How long would Celia live? How much time had he got? This was Elliot's chief concern. He kept up appearances, visiting her, chatting about the estate and the people who asked after her. He appeared loyal and seemed sad to see her as she had become. However, he was playing a waiting game - waiting for her passing.

When at Oakdene Manor he spent his time ransacking the place. He packed everything of value into boxes and stored them in the biggest out building. He then filled duplicate boxes with rubbish and locked them in a spare bedroom. If anyone asked where they were, Stephen, Lucille, possibly Anna he would say that, as the house was mostly unoccupied he felt safer if they were under lock and key, but fortunately nobody came to the house, not even Anna and the question was never asked, which suited his purposes very well.

Every time he visited his brother he would put as many boxes of stolen booty as he could into his new white van. These he took straight to his brother's house where they were sorted and distributed for sale.

Douglas had finished the last copy of a painting from Oakdene Manor and had put his business up for sale. When it was sold he would tell people that he was moving to Spain to open a gallery there. The two brothers already had a substantial *pot of gold* banked and at a moment's notice Elliot could transfer the rest. He would leave Oakdene depleted of nearly everything of value, including William's paintings which had been replaced by the copies that Douglas had painted, and an estate where some of the land had been sold for building or commercial purposes which was very remunerative and farms whose rent had been diverted directly into his pockets. Having managed to copy Anna's signature he had also laid his hands on most of William's savings.

He had not taken Stephen into his confidence, rather he had used him. He did feel guilty especially when he remembered his love for Evelyn, Stephen's mother, but he believed that Stephen was too honest, in fact, he knew that he questioned the legality of some of the things that Elliot had persuaded him to do, like sub letting land and pocketing the rents. He had not told him everything, not by a long shot and hoped that when he did finally disappear that Anna would allow Stephen and Lucille to continue with the caravan site, stables and farm. She may even properly install him as Estate Manager. What Stephen didn't know now, was to his benefit. But unfortunately things did not work out as Elliot had hoped that they would.

Stephen had started to be curious. He had been relieved when his father had said, "Forget your rent, Stephen," but it had left him dissatisfied. He had wanted to make a go of his farm, but profits were low. He had only been able to hire seasonal labour and had relied on Lucille to help financially with her growing riding stables. When Elliot had suggested that he find a more remunerative way of using his land and had suggested the caravan park Stephen had gone along with it and put his energies into the organisation of it. This took up his time and Elliott's other suggestion of sub-letting his fields had given him the freedom to do this. After the first year the caravan park was established and Lucille's growing children's farm had become immensely popular so much so that he spent his time helping her and not working for himself. Elliot had also suggested that he help with estate administration and had down loaded what Stephen needed to administer the everyday organisation of the estate onto Stephen's own computer.

There was therefore no need for Stephen to go to Oakdene Manor and to all intents and purposes the place was closed.

However one day Stephen was driving back home from another direction and needed to pass the Manor. He was surprised to see his father's white van parked in the courtyard when he had been told that he was visiting his brother Douglas in Bristol. A sudden urge made him turn into the drive and stop. He climbed out of his car and wandered towards the house, peeping as he passed into the van's open back doors. Boxes were piled up and some pieces of furniture. He could see the dismantled grandfather clock. His heart began to pound, his mind galloping horrifically at the possibility of what he was seeing.

He moved, quietly, into the kitchen, listening for sounds of activity.

He tiptoed into the hall and peeped round the door of the lounge. The emptiness of the place was obvious. The room contained only large pieces of furniture and was minus the grandfather clock and love seat. His father was holding one of the paintings. As he turned he caught sight of his son standing in the doorway. For a few seconds they stared at each other, then Stephen broke the silence saying,

"Dad, what are you doing? I can't believe it. This room is practically empty. Are you cleaning the place out?"

Elliot had no means of bluffing. His hardened face told it all.

"Guilty as charged."

"But why -- surely this will all be yours when Celia dies. You're her husband."

"I'm afraid not," said Elliot. "I found out after we were married that William had made it legally binding that Anna would inherit the estate."

"Would you have married Celia, if you'd known?"

"Probably not."

"So she didn't tell you, --- deliberately. She must love you very much."

Elliot gave a wry smile. "I care for her too, in my own

way, but - "

"---it was always her money that you wanted most," said Stephen.

"I wasn't meant to be poor, -- or even to work," Elliot said. "My father was as rich as Croesus, but he gambled it all away, and my mother was a whore, went off with the highest bidder. I knew what it was like to have money to spend until there wasn't any, so I decided to help myself."

"Dishonestly! By stealing," muttered Stephen. "So what are you going to do the next time Anna comes here?"

"She never comes. Celia won't live much longer. I'll stay for the funeral and then disappear. I'll be long gone before Anna and that snooty husband of hers finds out.

"What about me? Don't you care what happens to me, dad?" Stephen was becoming hysterical. "You're prepared to just clear off and forget me. Will I ever see you again? I suppose not. You've been missing half my life already. Why should I mind. You were never there when I needed you and now, when I thought we'd found each other again, you ----." He stumbled out of the room, tears not far away. He had no recollection of driving or of bursting in to his own home and throwing himself into a chair. His world had just collapsed around him and his look of desperation, when Lucille came rushing in, was almost too much to bear.

He clutched her so tightly that she could hardly breathe and all the time, sobbing, shrieking and rampaging against his father.

Finally he let her go and sank back into his chair. She knelt in front of him.

"Stephen! Stephen! Calm down. What's the matter?" She looked at his face, took in his misery and said gently, "Now tell me everything," --- and he did.

"So he married Celia for her money. I think we knew that really. However, they seemed so happy. She adores him. I wonder if she realised. She must have done. She's not stupid. I expect that's why she delayed in telling him that the estate would not be his. She was afraid he would leave her, or steal from her and she was right. Poor, lovely Celia. How can I visit her in the home now that I know all this? What if she lives on --- she could do? Will he hang around now that he's cleared out the place?"

"I don't think he'll be there for much longer -- now that I've seen what he's up to, and do you know, I don't care what he does anymore," said Stephen. "If it wasn't for you I'd have gone under. Your stables and children's farm has kept us going. I tried - worked my fingers to the bone in the early years but there was little profit in it and now we're left with this caravan park, suggested by him, and which the locals don't like and fields that are being farmed by others, which is probably against the tenancy agreement. I suppose he initiated me into the estate management in order to get himself out of it. Do you realise that, as soon as Anna and James find out they are going to come after us, believing that we were in on it, and how do I persuade them that I knew nothing at all about it?"

"We won't know where he's gone. Even if we found out where his brother's Art Gallery is, we'll probably discover that they're one step ahead of us, and will have disappeared leaving no trace. It makes me realise how little we knew the man," said Lucille," and what if Anna and James contact the Police. We'll be the first people that they question and they'll never believe that we knew nothing at all about what the brothers planned. I can't believe that your dad could be so cruel --- to his own son," and the emotion threatening her burst out in tears as the two clung to each other in the knowledge that their lives would never be the same again.

Elliot sat in the fading light with a glass of whisky in his hand and a grim expression on his face. He felt shaken. This confrontation with Stephen had been something that he had tried to avoid. He did not want to feel any emotion, to care or feel guilty at his actions, but there was a conscience within him rearing its ugly head manifesting itself in an awful feeling of shame. Stephen was his son and he had let him leave with the knowledge that all he cared for was money. He was right, of course.

However he was a villain and villains can't risk having feelings. He knew that he had one more task to do, where Stephen was concerned, which would, if discovered, be his son's downfall.

How could he do it? Because he had to. He had to implicate his son, to divert attention from himself, in order to allow him to disappear with Douglas and hide themselves away, without trace, in some far distant place which would most definitely not be Spain.

He had to wait his opportunity. He had been watching Beeches farm a lot lately, trying to decide the best time to enter the farmhouse when Stephen and Lucille were both out. A few days after the confrontation with Stephen he saw them both get into the Land Rover and drive away. He waited a short while, to make sure they didn't turn back, then drove down the lane and parked around the back, in the shadows. Out of his van he heaved two large flat parcels. He unlocked the front door and struggled with them up the stairs. He put the parcels down and went to fetch the hooked stick with which to pull open the loft hatch that was in the ceiling of the landing. Then he pulled down a stepladder and hoisted and pushed the two parcels up the ladder onto the dusty loft floor. He found a suitable place to hide them, at the far end under a lot of moth-eaten carpets, broken furniture and bits of junk. He quickly scattered a few old curtains on the floor to cover his footprints then beat a hasty retreat down and out of the house. The parcels would not be hard to find when the Police came looking.

He found himself shaking as he drove away.

Part 4

Chapter One

The second stroke had badly debilitated Celia. When she was moved to the home she spent the days sitting in a chair, watching the people around her. Her facial expressions were non-existent. She could make noises but not form words. She could use her one hand a little but the other had no strength or control in it to be of any use. When people called to see her she tried to smile but this caused her to dribble and when Anna or Elliot visited tears kept trickling down her cheeks.

Anna couldn't bear it. Her mother eventually found it difficult to even be spoon fed and gradually lost all the weight that she had gained after being immobilised from the first stroke. She developed bed sores and became so uncomfortable that she could only sit on a chair if it had a proper, therapeutic cushion on it. In this state they knew that she could not live much longer, in fact, Anna almost longed for her mother's suffering to be over,--- and one night this finally happened. She closed her eyes and fell asleep, never to wake again. Anna was heartbroken when she heard, even though she'd known that her mother would never improve.

Elliot, also felt unwanted emotion when the staff at the home rang him but his sorrow at her passing was nothing compared to the worry he now felt as he realised that this was it. Now matters needed to be finalised --- and quickly. Celia's death would put all sorts of wheels in motion and of necessity his time at Oakdene Manor must quickly come to an end. He would have to get away, leaving no trace of where he had gone, long before Anna walked through the door to take over her inheritance.

He arranged to meet her at the home the next day so that they could discuss funeral arrangements. He was determined to take charge and do all the organisation because he needed to persuade Anna not to open Oakdene Manor for the gathering of mourners after the funeral.

She was obviously distraught at her mother's death and clasped Elliot tightly, when they met, assuming that he felt the same.

"Oh, Elliott," she said, releasing him. "This is such a sad day. We're all going to miss her so very much."

The consummate actor within him put on a wonderful expression of grief, wiping his eyes, blowing his nose as he muttered how much she had meant to him and he didn't know how he was ever going to manage without her."

This started Anna off again and they both sat with their memories until a member of staff came in with some cups of tea.

"I suppose we'd better discuss the funeral," said Anna miserably.

"Would you like me to organise it?" asked Elliot. "I presume she'll be buried beside William in the churchyard of St. Giles. It's probably easier for me as I can also check up on the manor. It's been closed for a while now. It seemed so big and empty for me on my own, so I've stayed with Douglas, and Stephen and Lucille most of the time."

"Well, I was wondering whether to ask people back there. After all it was mum's home."

"The problem is," said Elliot, trying not to panic, "that the place needs a good warm up at this time of year and a thorough clean. We could employ caterers but they would only deal with food. I've no staff, now. There seems no point with just me there. I'm thinking that a hotel might be better because then everything could be provided, food and drink as well as comfortable rooms for anyone who needs to stay overnight.

"Well, perhaps you're right. After all it is November, but it's a shame that we can't all meet at the Manor again. I can remember my dad's funeral. The house looked splendid and the day was warm and sunny. So many people came from all over and were able to sit outside and enjoy the gardens. I realise that, now it's winter, being outside wouldn't have been possible, but I would have thought that there would have been plenty of room inside for people to sit, talk and remember mum. Any way if you think a hotel would be more comfortable and easier to organise then I'll go along with your decision. We'll get mum's funeral over with first before we open up Oakdene Manor and bring it to life again. It'll take some facing and I'm not sure I'm ready for that yet.

Elliot tried not to smirk at her words as he said, "I'll make some enquiries. There are several places in the near vicinity that might do. I did go, myself, to a funeral wake at a place called Ackworth Park which was very roomy and comfortable and the food was excellent."

This was a white lie. He'd dined there with Celia once and it was quite luxurious and, of course expensive. This time it would be Anna picking up the bill, so what did he care.

"I'll leave it with you then, Elliot. Let me know the details when you've made your decision. There are a lot of people who need to be informed. I'm very grateful to you and know you'll do your best for mum."

"Well, she was my wife, for a few years, anyway. I owe it to her to arrange things sensitively and properly," he said, turning away, leaving Anna the distinct impression that his eyes had filled with tears. As he reached for his hankie he grinned smugly, then turned and blew his nose, loudly.

So he did as he had promised. Everything was suitably arranged, the funeral director, church, hotel, and cars, and in this way the continued closure of Oakdene Manor was guaranteed.

Stephen and Lucille did not know that Celia had died until Lucille met Lucy Jones, the vicar's wife, in the local shop, a few days later.

"I would have popped round," she said, "to tell you but I thought Elliot or Anna would have done so."

"We haven't seen either of them for a while," said Lucille. This was not absolutely true, but she wasn't going to tell Lucy that.

"The funeral is going to be here in St. Giles church and Celia will be buried beside William in the churchyard. Afterwards they are inviting people to the Ackworth Park Hotel. I'm surprised at Anna going to that expense and not using Oakdene Manor," said Lucy.

I'm not, thought Lucille, *Elliot's idea, no doubt*, and saying goodbye to Lucy, hurried home to tell Stephen. It was obvious that Elliot had talked Anna into doing exactly what he wanted which was to keep her away from her inherited home.

Since that dreadful day when Stephen had become aware of Elliot's awful duplicity, he and Lucille had been constantly trying to work out how they were going to survive, without being considered involved too. Anna and James and all the village would assume, as Elliot was Stephen's father, that they must have known what he'd been planning.

Lucille was all for going straight to the Police to inform on him. She was incensed that he had been so callous towards Stephen and so wickedly scheming. Stephen had restrained her, "We must be careful, think ahead, Lucille. It will be better to keep a low profile and let Anna contact the Police when she finds out what has happened. We don't want to put ourselves in the spotlight. The police will go to look round the Manor, with Anna and James and will see instantly what's been going on. Anna will be asked about dad and we're certain to be mentioned and then they'll come knocking. I expect we'll be the first on their list."

"We'll deny everything. Say that we've not been near the place or seen Elliot for weeks," said Lucille. "After all it is almost the truth."

"Yes, but he's been living here with us, on and off, since Celia went into the Home, although we haven't seen much of him lately, and let's face it I did see what he was doing that day and I'll have to tell them."

"They'll not believe you, Stephen, but, I agree, we'll keep quiet and only speak up when questioned."

So nothing had been decided, and then they'd heard the news of Celia's death. Stephen had been adamant that he was not going to the funeral. There was no way he was going to witness the display that his father would put on for the benefit of all the relatives and other guests. Lucille wanted to attend, however. Celia had been a good friend and she owed it to her memory to put her hatred of Elliot aside for an hour, and mourn her.

Their biggest problem when the funeral was over would be totally out of their control. It was the question of how long they had before Anna and James unlocked the door of Oakdene Manor and saw the state of the place for themselves. It would be then that they would realise why Elliot had steered Anna away from opening the house up for the funeral tea.

"It'll be a rude awakening for them," said Lucille, "when they discover how they've been fooled by your father."

"I'll give them a day or two, but it won't be long," said Stephen. "I should imagine that everything of any value will have gone, as will my father. I doubt that any of us will see or hear from him again."

"They are going to have a terrible shock," said Lucille. Just imagine going into your home, or a place really familiar and finding that it has been ransacked. Poor Anna, she's going to be devastated and all this on top of losing her mother."

"Then the Police will come after us," said Stephen. How am I going to convince them that I had nothing to do with it? How naive we've been. We suspected him - suspected that not everything he did was actually legal but I was desperate to make ends meet and now I'll probably be accused of being in it with him. I might even be arrested," and he threw himself desperately into a chair "What a mess, -- what a b----- awful mess," he stormed.

Chapter Two

The funeral was over. The roadside had been lined with villagers standing quietly in respect, as the hearse, covered with flowers, went by. Celia had been well-known and her open friendly personality had warmed the hearts of many people. After the service in St. Giles church, Elliot walked with Anna behind the coffin to the burial place that had been prepared for her, next to William, in the churchyard.

He could feel his heart beating frantically, not because of the great sorrow of the occasion but for quite another reason. For the moment he must stand as the distressed widower and accept the pity and condolences from Celia's friends and relatives, appearing sad and bewildered at the loss of the wife that he had been married to for just a few short years. He would bide his time with apparent solemnity until he could safely leave, plead his need for solitude, and make his escape.

Thus, alongside Anna, James and Adam, he bowed his head, stood by the grave and watched with a solemn face as the coffin was lowered and the final interment prayers were said. Then he threw down a red rose as a loving gesture to his beloved wife.

There was no sarcasm in this action. He had cared for her, in his own way, but liked what she could give him, more. He was certain that he had made her happy and loved her as much as he was able. He had been playing a game of patience, worming his way into her affections and those of her family but all the time probing and questioning until the day that he had finally discovered the truth, --- that he would not inherit Oakdene Manor nor would he be left any money. An annual allowance (albeit a generous one) was not what he was after and from that moment his journey for revenge had begun.

After a few quiet moments around the grave, when all that could be heard was Anna's muffled sobs, they all turned to move away.

"I'm not coming to the hotel immediately," he said. "I want to stay here, with Celia for a while, and then, later I'm going away for a few days, somewhere peaceful where I can gather my thoughts and decide what to do next. My brother has offered me a home with him - but he has his own life to lead and I've imposed on him far too much, lately."

Anna could see how upset Elliot was, as he wiped his eyes. She didn't say anything. Her own emotions were hard enough for her to deal with but she moved forward and hugged him. Then he shook hands with James and Adam, turning to watch them as they walked along the churchyard path towards their waiting car.

He stood looking down at the oak coffin in which his dead wife lay.

This time real tears oozed out of his eyes. He brushed them away, annoyed at his emotion.

"Goodbye, Celia," he said, "I wish things could have been different," and finally, pulling himself together turned and hurried away feeling glad that Celia had not seen how he had dealt with Oakdene Manor as a result of her decision to leave it all to Anna. He reached the place where he had parked his car - no longer the van but a hired replacement, and without looking back, he drove away.

The following Saturday Anna, James and Adam got up early to drive to Oakdene Manor. Anna was nervously excited. It was a long time since they'd been there and they knew that it would feel cold and unlived in as they'd understood that Elliot had closed it down during the period that Celia had been in the Nursing home. They'd had little time to worry about the house, believing it was in good hands and, of course, her mother's needs had come first.

Elliot had given them the keys when they met at the funeral and Anna was both elated and sad as she sat in the car beside James. She had finally inherited her old home. She knew it would be a poignant experience when she walked in through the door, now that both her beloved parents had gone, but never did she imagine that the emotion she would feel would be completely different to the one she had expected.

"The first thing we'll do is put the heating on," Anna said, as she walked from the car towards the kitchen. "It'll be freezing inside."

She unlocked the door, opened it and reached to switch on the light. The kitchen looked so sad and unused and smelt fusty from being closed up. She looked around, seeing the familiar things, the Aga, large table and old comfy chair, but the worktops and dresser looked decidedly bare and there was a dirty square on the floor where the fridge should have been.

"That's strange," she said. "Elliot didn't mention that the fridge had broken down. I thought it was a fairly new one."

"I'll see to the heating," said James, crossing to the utility room. He turned on the light and then stopped in the doorway.

"My god!" he said. Anna and Adam rushed across to see what was wrong. They were faced with a noticeably empty space. Gone was the washing machine, drier and large chest freezer.

"See to the heating, James," she said, with a grave face, "then we'd better check the house. I've got a horrible feeling about this."

With Adam she moved into the hall. They were eventually followed by James. What they saw was an inheritor's worst nightmare. A great many things, small and large, were missing. Everything of value seemed to have gone. They walked from room to room. The paintings were no longer there, the large TV, selective pieces of furniture and the valuable grandfather clock. Drawers had been emptied, the bureau had been rifled, some photographs remained in cheap frames, mirrors and clocks removed.

Upstairs, was much the same and Celia's bedroom, especially, had been methodically emptied and her most expensive clothes and jewellery were all gone.

Anna collapsed on the bed, sobbing her heart out.

"What's happened? I don't understand."

"We've been burgled. Systematically cleaned out," said James, "and I don't think we need to look far to find out who by."

Anna looked up, through her tears at the face of her husband. Anger was beginning to take hold of him.

"It's him! Elliot! He's taken us for fools, standing by your mum's grave, earning our sympathy and respect when all the time laughing at us, knowing what he'd done and what we would find here. No wonder he didn't want to hang around."

"Why -- why did he do it? I thought he loved my mum," said Anna. "Obviously he loved money more," said James, "and certainly cared nothing for us. We should have trusted to our initial instincts. We were right from the start. He only ever wanted your mum's money and this is his reaction when he discovered that he wasn't going to get it."

Anna sobbed and trembled with the horror of it and James sat down beside her and took her in his arms.

Adam, who had been inspecting the rest of the house came in and said,

"He has still been living here, mum. There's an unmade bed and some dirty cups in the back bedroom, and along the landing one of the rooms is locked."

"Perhaps he's stored things in there, for safety, as the house was empty," said Anna hopefully. "Maybe we've judged him before knowing the full picture."

They hurried to the locked room and tried the door then searched the house, but could find no keys.

"He's thrown them away," said James. "I'm going to break the door down." "Stand back." It wasn't easy. The door was strong, but eventually with Adam's help they managed to open it and look inside.

"It's full of boxes," said James, and started to open one

of them. He rifled in amongst the bubble wrap and paper. There was nothing else in the box. After opening several more that they found filled with newspapers, sand, carrier bags, supermarket empties it was obvious that this collection had been created just in case anyone, particularly themselves, had called unexpectedly and asked questions about the missing items. They could almost hear Elliot say, "They are packed away in boxes in a spare room, for safe keeping."

James was, by now, absolutely furious. He stormed out of the room full of empty boxes saying," I'm calling the Police, straight away."

"What about Stephen," asked Adam? "I wonder if he knew what his father was doing. Do you think he's involved?"

"He must have known what was going on," said James. "He only lives just down the road."

"--- and Lucille. What about her? I thought she was mum's friend," cried Anna.

"It's possible, I suppose that he kept them in the dark. However I think we should pay them a visit," said James." See what they've got to say for themselves."

"Then there's the bank. He's obviously clever enough to have emptied the accounts," said Adam. "Probably forged your signature, mum."

Anna gasped. "Ring the Police, James. Tell them what's happened and get them here quickly. Ask them to ring your mobile when they're on their way. See how long they expect to be. Meanwhile we'll all go and call on the Marshalls'," said Anna.

Stephen and Lucille had been trying to prepare for this moment. Lucille, working in the kitchen heard and saw the car first as it drove into their yard.

"Stephen! Stephen, they're here."

She opened the door to a grim faced trio.

"Come in," said Lucille, quietly, and ushered them into their sitting room.

Stephen joined them and they all sat down.

"I --we've just had a terrible shock," said Anna, threatening to cry.

"It appears that Oakdene Manor has been ransacked," said James solemnly -- we're assuming by your father, who we have all grown to trust and who, given the evidence before us has taken everything he could lay his hands on. Before we speak to the Police we want you to tell us what you know. As his son, they'll certainly want to question you, to see if you're involved."

Stephen looked worried. "Of course I'm not," he said. "He fooled us, just the same as you." They could see the moisture of anxiety glistening on his forehead. Restlessly he stood up and started pacing the room.

"It was only last week that I realised how little I knew my father, and since then I have gone from shock and horror to raging anger. If it wasn't for Lucille I -- well I don't know what I would have done."

He sat and held Lucille's hand as he told the story that had completely changed his attitude towards his father.

"We hadn't seen dad for some time. We believed that he had closed the house down and was supposedly spending his time with my uncle. This, it seems was only part of the truth. He was still spending a lot of time at the Manor. He'd acquired a white van, having sold the large car that he used to transport Celia in. He said the van belonged to Uncle Douglas.

I was driving home last Wednesday from North Leech---- a direction that I don't often take. It took me past Oakdene Manor and as I passed I looked up the drive and caught a glimpse of the van parked in the courtyard, so I thought, as dad was there, I'd go and say *hello*. I left the car in the drive and as there was no sign of dad I wandered towards the van and, seeing the back doors open, I glanced inside. It was piled with boxes, small pieces of furniture, some lamps and the dismantled grandfather clock. I can tell you my heart started to beat frantically as I wondered what was going on. I crept in through the kitchen door, following the sounds into the hall and across to the lounge. As I told Lucille, I saw dad on a stool lifting down the Dunstable landscape painting that hung above the hearth. As he turned he saw me. His face was fearsome, his glance almost evil. We had words, well I ended up shouting. I did not want to believe what I was seeing nor what he was admitting to, without any remorse at all. I ran out, raced home and---"

"He threw himself into a chair," said Lucille. "I've never seen such misery and horror on his face before. He clutched me and sobbed, uncontrollably for a minute or so. When he did calm down enough for me to get some sense out of him, he told me what he'd seen. We have spent the time since then in limbo, knowing that we must inform you but dreading having to, and we have been mulling over the last few years, coming to the realisation that we didn't know him at all."

"You'll know that I grew up without him," said Stephen. " There's no doubt that he loved my mother but when she died he drifted away, spent more and more time with his brother. I was lucky that my grandparents took me over. I had a good education and they helped to set me up here. They're getting old now. Their farm is run by my uncles. Grandad and Gran would be horrified if they knew the sort of man their son-in-law really is.

You see, I've never known much about his upbringing except that his parents were wealthy. He used to tell me stories about his life in a large house with many servants. He told me of how he and Uncle Douglas would peer through the banisters at fabulously dressed men and women, wining, dining and dancing.

That was until they were sent away to school, and when they came home one holiday their mother had gone and they never saw or heard from her again. It was only later that he learnt about his father, that he had gambled away his money and committed suicide. We were shocked when he told us this one night, but he never opened up about how he earned a living. I know he had an interest in cars and kept all the farm vehicles serviced when he lived with my mother, but after that his life is actually a mystery.

He was very secretive. I was astounded when he turned up in a Land Rover for me as a 21st birthday present, and pleased when he seemed to enjoy staying with Lucille and I and working with us on the farm. But he always kept drifting away, that is until he met your mum, Celia. Then he became a permanent fixture and you know the rest."

"We had a few happy years together before and after they were married," said Lucille. "Celia and I became good friends. She was like a mother figure to me. We got on so well and she loved working with the horses. I think - thought that she and Elliot were very happy. They settled down together at Oakdene Manor and it was obvious that Elliot liked being in charge of the estate. Now, of course, we realise that he believed it would all be his, on her death, and Celia did not let him know any different not until she had to. I think she knew what he wanted but so long as he was ignorant of the inheritance they were happy, and thinking about it, had she not met Elliot she would have become a lonely old lady. As it was she had a few years of fulfilment, travelling, holidays, living a full and exciting life and she blossomed in the company of a man who could be kind and caring."

"Well," said James, "we were all hoodwinked, then, and now we'll be lucky if there is a penny left."

His phone suddenly rang and when he answered, got up, ready to go. "The Police are on their way. We'd better hurry."

"Do you have the estate laptop?" Adam asked. "We need to study it."

"I haven't been using it. I assume dad still has it and has taken it with him. The one I use is mine," said Stephen. "Dad just downloaded the files that I needed to administer the Estate business."

"Ah," said James. "He's thought of everything."

As the three of them walked to the door James said to Stephen, "You'd better brace yourselves for a bumpy ride. I think things will get worse before they get better."

Chapter Three

Anna, James and Adam returned to Oakdene Manor and waited only a short while until the police arrived. When the two plain clothes policemen knocked on the door James opened it and inspected their ID's. They then followed him into the lounge. The older, a rather short, tubby man with a lazy air but sharp, bright eyes, introduced himself as Inspector Whitcombe. His assistant was a taller, younger lady with a pleasant smile. She carried a large handbag from which she removed a camera and notepad. James offered them some window seats around the large bay window. There were no chairs at all in the room. Then he fetched kitchen chairs for himself and Anna. So the two members of the police settled with their backs to the window facing Anna and James and were able to look around the room and note its bareness.

"This is Sergeant Dickenson," the Inspector said. "She will be making notes and taking photographs. I believe you wish to report a burglary."

"My house has been ransacked, Inspector," said Anna, bristling at his nonchalance. "Everything that could be easily moved has gone, and the value of the missing items is considerable."

No amount of censure rattled the composure of this hardened policeman. He rose to his feet saying, "Right then, Mrs. Sheppard, we'd better look around, and you can tell us what is missing."

This was not a quick process. Photographs were taken of the rooms especially where it was obvious that items had stood or been hung, but gradually as they proceeded round the house, the evidence was sadly very clear. The whole place had been completely stripped of its most valuable possessions.

By the end Anna was visibly distraught. The Inspector, not an uncaring man, suggested that they all sit down over a cup of tea and sort out what to do next. Anna had brought a few provisions, knowing that there would be little in the house and James and Adam managed to rustle up some refreshments whilst Sergeant Dickenson sat with Anna in the lounge, speaking softly as she offered comfort.

Whilst the tea was being made the Inspector went outside and had a quick look around, taking note of the size of the house, quadrangle of buildings around the yard and the extensive gardens.

Mm, he thought, a valuable property. Somebody knew what they were doing. Time to find out who, and he returned inside to join the waiting group. Accepting a cup of tea he sat down to begin his questioning. As Anna still looked upset he began with James.

"Mr. Sheppard, do you have any idea who may be responsible for this burglary?" asked the Inspector. He wasn't surprised that there was an immediate positive response. In his experience you didn't have to look far from home to solve most crimes.

"Of course we do," said James. "His name is Elliot Marshall, my mother-in-law's second husband, and he seems to have taken us for everything we possess. My wife, Anna has only recently inherited Oakdene Manor on the death of her mother, Celia. Her first husband, William, had bequeathed it to her for her lifetime and on her death to Anna.

Celia met Elliot about eleven years ago. His son, Stephen, is one of the estates' tenant farmers and he was staying with him and his wife, Lucille.

We weren't too sure about him from the beginning but he eventually won us over. He was ten years younger than Celia, but he seemed to make her happy. Anna and I both have busy jobs, Anna had become a head teacher and myself a hospital consultant. We were glad that Celia was happy again and not so lonely and dependant on us and we accepted the situation quite readily when they got married.

Sadly about five years ago Celia had a stroke and although she initially came home, she had another one a few years later and eventually had to be moved to a nursing home where she recently died.

Elliot appeared to be the perfect husband. He had the house altered for Celia's needs and visited her regularly when she was in the nursing home.

"Did he expect to inherit the estate?" the Inspector asked.

"I'm sure of it," said James. " Elliot loved being Lord of the Manor, taking over the running of it and I have to admit that the estate prospered."

"My mother didn't actually lie to him about the fact that I was to have Oakdene Manor when she died," said Anna, " but it took him a long time to dare to ask if she had made a will in his favour. When she came clean and explained the situation, she thought she'd lost him as he became quiet and very moody."

"He has a brother, in Bristol," said James," and he visits him a lot. For a while he went there, but he did eventually come back, bright as a button and seemingly just as before, but I think it was during this visit that the two of them devised what I believe is the dastardly plot that has landed us in this awful position. I have a feeling that when we delve into all the finances and investments, we are going to find that he has taken nearly all of them.

Unfortunately, when Celia became ill Anna agreed that he could have joint Power of Attorney and I'm certain that he was clever enough to forge her signature, in many cases, so that he had could do just as he pleased."

"Right then," said the Inspector, briskly. "Can you supply me with a photograph of Mr. Marshall, and his brother?"

"We don't have many, but there's this one," said Anna, crossing to the piano where she'd placed the smashed photo frame that held the images of her smiling mother and an equally happy Elliot, on their wedding day. "There was an album, but we'll have to look for that, if it's still here."

"We'll send a team in to search the house thoroughly

and take fingerprints. We'll need them from yourselves and anyone else who has come in and out of this house, over the last few years, staff, friends, relatives. This is for elimination purposes. Also we need the room that you believe Elliot slept in, untouched. We can get DNA and fingerprints from the dirty cups. I also require the address of his brother, Douglas."

Anna looked worried as she glanced at James.

"We don't know it Inspector. We never have. We've met his brother only once at mum's wedding, but we've always known that he ran an Art Gallery. He was apparently a talented artist.

"Is the gallery in Bristol?"

"Yes, we believe so," said James.

"Then we'll find it."

They got up to leave.

"We must get this photograph distributed to all the airports and local police forces," said the inspector, "although I'm afraid several days have passed since your mother's funeral and Mr. Marshall and his brother are probably long gone by now. I'll send a forensic team out on Monday. Will someone be here?"

"Yes, we'll make sure we are," said Anna. "We'll be going home tonight as tomorrow we'll need to organise our jobs to free us up for a while. It'll not be easy especially for James. However we've inherited a situation that no-one could have imagined. The thought of that man getting away with - well treating my mother's memory so callously - it's - so - awful."

James put his arm round her as the tears began to flow.

"Take heart," said the inspector. "Villains like him nearly always slip up somewhere and when they do we'll be waiting."

The next day for Anna meant a long talk with the Chairman of the School Governors and a visit to her deputy, who would have to take over from her, at least until the end of term. They were shocked at her sudden departure but promised their support in any way they could. Fay, her deputy, always practical, could see the shock on Anna's face and told her not to worry about school. They'd all cope, but she was sorry that Anna was missing all the Christmas festivities that both staff and pupils enjoyed.

"James and I have always known that we would retire to Oakdene Manor one day, " said Anna, "and run the estate, but hoped that it was still in the distant future, but over the last few years with mum being ill we knew that the time was coming closer. However, this disaster we did not foresee and I'm probably going to be resigning straight away because of it."

"We'll miss you," said Fay, emotionally as they hugged each other.

"I've a long, desperate road in front of me, "said Anna.

"I know. It'll be tough," said Fay. "You will keep in touch. Let us know how you are getting on? "

"Of course," said Anna, kissing her goodbye. "I must admit I'd rather be turning up for school tomorrow than doing something as unpleasant as trying to sort this mess out."

James could not cancel his appointments so easily and spent most of the week trying to re-arrange and download his work onto others. He did inform the Board that he would be resigning and they were sympathetic and shocked when they heard why.

Adam spoke to his tutors and was able to work via the Internet for a while. He helped Anna pack up what they needed for a few days, food clothes etc. and ordered a fridge/freezer to be delivered to Oakdene Manor as soon as possible. Then in the late afternoon the two of them travelled back not at all relishing what lay ahead.

On the Monday Anna would be contacting her mother's solicitor in the hope that there would be some light shown on what was insured, stored in the bank and, of course to look at her mother's will. She was glad that James had helped her compile the list of valuables in the house, when

Elliot first came on the scene, and sighed at how they had ignored the signs and not followed their initial instincts. When you've not mixed with people like him before it's hard to accept that they exist.

The answer phone was flashing when they got in and, switching it on, they listened to a rather mysterious message.

"This is Sir Ian Townsend speaking. I have the deposit ready for you, Mr. Marshall. Will you contact me and let me know your arrangements for its transfer. My number is ------. Goodbye."

"A deposit for what?" said Anna gasping.

"Leave this to me, mum," said Adam. "I'll ring back and find out what this is all about."

He dialled the number and a woman answered.

"May I speak to Sir Ian Townsend please."

"I'm afraid he's out at the moment. I'm his wife, Lady May. Can you tell me what it's about?"

"My name is Adam Sheppard and Sir Ian has left a message on my phone, ---something about a deposit for a Mr. Elliot Marshall."

"Oh," said Lady May, "Sir Ian must have dialled the wrong number."

"I don't think so," said Adam. "Elliot Marshal did live here, but he has now gone. Can I ask what it is that you are wanting to put a deposit on?"

"Why Oakdene Manor, of course. He has agreed to sell it to us."

Adam paled. From the message, he'd half expected this. He looked at his mother. If she'd lost Oakdene as well, she would have been devastated. It seemed that they'd found out about this sale in the nick of time.

"I'm sorry to tell you, Lady May, that Oakdene Manor is not for sale. It is not Elliot Marshall's to sell. It belongs to my mother who has recently inherited it. I'm afraid all Elliot Marshall's dealings with you are fraudulent."

"Oh, no," gasped Lady May.

"Keep your money in the Bank. It seems that you've had a lucky escape," said Adam. "He would have pocketed it and disappeared."

"Who is he, then?" asked Lady May.

"He was my grandmother's second husband and we now believe that he married her for her money and the Oakdene Estate. Obviously, as her husband, he expected to inherit it, after her death, but he later found out that her first husband, my Grandad had made a will leaving everything to my mother, as their only daughter and then to myself. Since finding this out he has been scheming and helping himself to whatever he could. A couple of weeks ago my grandmother died and we are now beginning to uncover everything that he has done. The police have been informed and we'll now hope that they will find him and lock him up. After my grandmother's funeral he disappeared, and when we found the state in which he has left Oakdene Manor we are, naturally horrified and very angry. My mother is extremely distraught,"

" --- as am I," said Lady May."I was so excited about buying such a beautiful house. Please accept our apologies for causing her even more distress."

"Thankyou I will. Goodbye."

Adam put the phone down and looked at his mother.

"You don't need to tell me," said Anna, shivering. "He tried to sell Oakdene Manor as well."

Chapter Four

"He'd never have managed to sell the house, and pocket all the money" said James to Anna, over the phone, after she'd rung to inform him of this latest development, "but he could easily have got the deposit. The sheer value of the house and estate must amount to millions and with any house it takes time for all the details to be finalised. It was lucky that you heard the message. If your mum hadn't died when she did, but in a few weeks time Elliot would have answered and replied to it, and probably have come into possession of a huge sum of money. I must say that Sir Ian and Lady May have had a very lucky escape."

"As have we," said Anna. "It's just another terrible shock to cope with. I'm glad Adam was here with me, to help. We should have expected it. If Elliot was not going to inherit Oakdene then his next best option was obviously to try and sell it. He wanted absolutely everything and he very nearly got it. Oh, James, things seem to be getting worse. Can anything else go wrong?"

James sensed how emotional Anna was. "Sit down with a strong drink and relax. I'll be up as soon as I can, tomorrow. I can't say that I'm looking forward to facing up to the full knowledge of what Elliot has stolen. The worst thing is going to be finding out what, if anything, you have got left."

Adam spent the evening investigating the estate website. He'd decided to visit all the tenant farmers and find out everything he could about their dealings with Elliot, and to encourage them to keep going, not involve the press and be confident that his parents, the new owners would deal with them with consideration.

Anna, after the day's shattering events took herself to bed early but did not sleep as her mind kept mulling over all the things that Elliot had done or tried to do.

James arrived after lunch to a house in turmoil. A forensic

team had arrived. The house was being searched for evidence. No place escaped their scrutiny. A smile had come on Anna's face when a full box was discovered in the room piled with empty ones. The box revealed, not rubbish, but some of her mother's cutlery and china.

"One box that he forgot to take, Mrs. Sheppard," said one of the white coated policemen, grinning.

They had all gone by early afternoon, but, as James and Anna left for their meeting with the solicitor, they noticed a gang of pressmen hovering at the gate, cameras ready.

"Oh, no," said Anna, trying to hide her face.

"It doesn't take them long to sniff out a story," muttered James.

Evan Pugh had been William's solicitor from the time that he had bought Oakdene Manor. He was a quiet-voiced, sympathetic man and today realised that he needed all his years of experience in facing the unpleasant task of sorting out Anna and James' problems.

His secretary brought in some tea, then Anna explained briefly what had recently happened. Evan Pugh remembered Celia's transactions with him before she married her second husband, Elliot, and that he'd drawn up a legal document, whereby he would receive a generous annuity after her death.

He produced this document and Celia's will, which confirmed that she had left all her estate to Anna and then to Adam. The codicil, added after her marriage to Elliot, gave him a very generous amount of money, annually.

"Well that's not going to happen," said Anna, fiercely. "In any case he's disappeared so, unless he shows up, that's it. He's already taken us for everything that he could lay his hands on and I hope the police will arrest him as soon as he makes an appearance, if he ever does."

Anna had only explained her situation, briefly, over the phone, whilst making an appointment and now enlightened Mr. Pugh with the whole story. In all his working life he had never come across such a deliberate example of greed and treachery. He was astounded and shocked by Anna's revelation and rather surprised, although he didn't say so, that they had been so easily taken in. Anna and James were intelligent people although they had been suspicious from the first, but their concern over Celia's health had been their priority and the care and solicitousness of Elliot had obviously seemed to them to be perfectly genuine.

Attached to the will were lists that William had added of his investments, properties and businesses owned, and the dates that they were sold and how much money was realised when he retired to Oakdene Manor. There was also information on where the money was saved and all his accounts, bonds etc. This would all have to be investigated but they were now prepared to discover that these had all been cashed in. Elliot would have been able to find out this information and withdraw the money, signing on behalf of Celia and putting it elsewhere under one of his fictitious names.

Then there was the list of paintings, their purchase price and how much they were insured for which was, most probably, not enough as they were worth millions.

"So all of the paintings are gone, Mrs. Sheppard?"

"Yes, and all the property that we itemised when mum and Elliot got married."

"I have the list here," said Evan Pugh. "I'll pass this on to the Police and hope that some of it turns up again."

Anna, near to tears again, said, "It isn't that I hanker for all mum's money, but I feel so much to blame for all of this. Dad would have sussed him out in a minute, and we were very aware of what he could be, but mum was so happy that we relaxed and welcomed him into our family. What fools we were. Such utter fools!" and silence fell on the office for a moment whilst the outcome of this tragedy filled their minds.

Breaking the misery Evan Pugh pushed back his chair and stood up, as did Anna and James. "I'll keep in touch, Mrs. Sheppard," he said as they shook hands, "and try to search for the positive. At least you have your mother's beautiful house."

"But he tried to sell that, too," said James, "and nearly got away with it."

Adam's day was surprising rather than anything else. Surprising in the fact that all the tenant farmers had had a great relationship with Elliot.

"It's obvious," he said later, to his parents, "that the man was a superb actor. He won them all over, offering help, with their vehicle maintenance --- for which he charged far less than they would have had to pay elsewhere, and not putting up their rent.

What they didn't know was that all they paid him was going straight into his pockets and he kept them onside so that they would keep paying without complaint.

When I told them that he had left, they were surprised, but I didn't tell them why although they looked curious. They'll have assumed it was something to do with Grandma's death, but I didn't enlighten them. They'll have to wait until the truth finally comes out. I did assure them that everything would continue as usual, that their tenancies were secure. Let's hope I'm right."

"How did you get on with Stephen?" Anna asked.

"The man's a total wreck, I'm afraid," said Adam. "I couldn't help feeling sorry for him as I listened, but annoyed at his stupidity, all down to his crook of a father who changed his world completely when he came back on the scene, making promises and suggestions."

"It's a pity for him that he did," said James. "Stephen would have worked hard all his life with Lucille's support,---- in an honest fashion, but his father turned up, offering gifts, a Land Rover, and help on the farm, and Stephen got the impression that he wanted to rebuild the father-son relationship that they had had when he was much younger, before his mother died."

"He admitted that the few years that they'd had after Elliot had met Grandma and then married her were happy," said Adam. "Her involvement with Lucille's riding school and Elliot's help with the estate had made him feel that they were building a settled future, but as soon as Grandma had her stroke and was disabled, things changed."

Stephen said that Elliot had started spending more time with his brother and because of this he struggled again, so when his father saw this he suggested that he opened a caravan park and sublet fields, so that someone else worked them instead of him. Doing this had been the last straw in keeping their heads above water.

However, Stephen admitted in this last year that he hadn't seen his dad much at all. In fact it all fell into place when he discovered him emptying the house. I'm afraid his eyes have been opened and he's absolutely devastated. Lucille is trying to help him cope but they both appear terribly shocked especially Stephen who realises that Elliot's life revolved completely around himself and that he cared very little for anyone else."

"Don't sympathise with him too much Adam," said James, cynically. "He is his father's son, after all, and may not prove to be as innocent as he makes out. Anyway the police are sure to question him, and what they find out will be very interesting."

Chapter Five

The knock on the door was loud and purposeful. When Stephen answered it he was faced with the two CID officers that had previously called at the Manor. They showed him their ID cards.

"Are you Mr. Stephen Marshall?"

"Yes," said Stephen hesitantly.

"I'm Inspector Whitcombe," announced the man, "and this is Sergeant Dickinson. We are here concerning the theft of valuable items from Oakdene Manor and to establish whether you know anything about the disappearance of a Mr. Elliot Marshall, your father I believe."

Stephen ushered them in, closing the door with shaking hands. He called Lucille and they all sat down in the sitting room. The Inspector looked around at a room that attempted brightness but appeared slightly shabby with furniture that had definitely seen better days. Then he turned his sharp bird-like eyes on his prey, a young man with fear written all over his face and a wife, flashily dressed with loyalty shining from her eyes.

"Mr. Marshall, we are here to question you and find out what you know about your father's affairs," said the Inspector.

"Well -- not a lot, really," said Stephen, and wringing his hands muttered, "He a-appears to have walked out on us again. We s-served our purpose, helping him cultivate a relationship with Celia, at the Manor and now, apparently, as you obviously suspect, he has - er - stolen everything worth any value from there, leaving Anna and James practically penniless, I believe --- and d- deserting me."

"Can you tell me about him?" asked the Inspector.

"As much as I can," said Stephen. We were a happy family until my mother died. I was just a kid but my father left me to live with my grandparents. So you see I don't really know him. He turned up a few years ago on my 21st birthday with a Land Rover as a present. I was stunned but thrilled. I thought that it meant that he wanted me back in his life especially as we seemed to get on so well and when I took on this tenancy he stayed with us for long spells of time and helped us on the farm, but Celia's illness and death changed him. I believe he thought that, as Celia's husband he would inherit Oakdene Manor and estate and also have all Celia's money to spend, --- which was probably the only reason he married her."

"Well it does seem like that," said the Inspector, getting up, but I'm afraid we must search your house and the bedroom that he used, Mr. Marshall because he lived with you for long periods of time and may have left some clues. Two officers are outside waiting to start."

"What are you looking for?" asked Stephen worriedly.

"Anything incriminating," said Inspector Whitcombe, "after all he appears to have broken the law and he may have left things here that will help us to find him and prove his guilt."

They had no choice but to allow them in. The Police started a thorough search of every part of the house and farm, even places that were disused and obviously neglected. Stephen and Lucille could only watch and wait, drink tea and try not to worry. They were hopeful as the day progressed that nothing would be found. Their one certainty was that they would be left with a lot of mess to clear up.

Suddenly there was loud shouting and movement from upstairs. Lucille dashed into the hall and looked up. She saw that the loft hatch was open and the ladder down.

"Stephen," she muttered. "They're in the loft." Stephen hurriedly joined her and they both watched as a policeman emerged and started climbing down the ladder. At the bottom he turned and reached up towards another officer who was framed in the hatchway. Then they saw a large, parcel wrapped up tightly being passed down from one to the other. This was followed by another. The second policeman then climbed down the ladder, folded it inside the loft and closed the hatch. They then carried the parcels down the stairs, passing Stephen and Lucille, and set them down in the kitchen on the table. One started to unwrap them whilst the other called Inspector Whitcombe on his mobile, who had been sitting, with Sergeant Dickinson in his car.

Stephen, looking worried, whispered to Lucille,

"What have they got there? I've never seen those two parcels before. I didn't put them in the loft, did you?

Lucille shook her head.

"We rarely go up there. Whatever can be inside them," she said fearfully.

They stood as if transfixed, not daring to move as they watched. Things did not look good for them. The Police had found something in their house, that they knew nothing about and could probably incriminate them.

Inspector Whitcombe and Sergeant Dickenson arrived and stood peering at the parcels as they were unwrapped. They then turned and looked at the couple silhouetted in the doorway. Their expressions were serious and the Inspector's manner distinctly unfriendly.

"Mr. Marshall," he said. "We have found these. Will you look at them and tell us what they are and why they have been found hidden in your loft?"

Stephen started to shake as he moved, followed by Lucille, to see what the parcels contained.

"Do not touch anything, please," said the Sergeant, indicating to the young policeman, who was wearing gloves, that he should spread the contents out.

Stephen and Lucille found themselves staring at a group of six paintings, that looked old and valuable. They knew immediately that they were from the Manor. They'd seen them many times, hanging in various places around the house when they'd visited and knew how proud Celia had been of them. William, her first husband had invested a great deal of money into this collection.

"Th-- th--- ey 're from Oakdene Manor," stuttered

Stephen. "William's valuable collection of paintings. It was the one of these that I saw my father taking down one day, but-- but what are they doing in my loft? We rarely go up there." He glanced at Lucille, fear etching his face. " It's my father. He's put them there, hasn't he -- to make us look guilty. He wants me to go to prison - - He must hate me very much," and, clutching Lucille, he sank onto a chair, with a desperate look of horror on his face.

Lucille, trying to help him turned to the Inspector and said, "We know nothing of this, honestly we don't. Elliot's set us up, planting these valuable paintings where he knew they would be found quite easily. Trying to pass the blame onto us. He probably found the paintings too hot to handle. You must believe me Inspector. We didn't know they were there."

It was hopeless. They knew it. The evidence was for all to see.

"Stephen Marshall," said the Inspector, formally. "I arrest you for the possession of stolen property -----."

"No, no, I didn't take them. I don't know ----," shouted Stephen as he was handcuffed and taken away.

Lucille shrieked, "No, no, -- he didn't -- do it," as she rushed out after him, but it was no good. There was nothing she could do to stop them arresting Stephen, and she stood, all alone in the yard, watching as they drove away, tears pouring down her face as she tried to work out what to do next.

She rang her father and mother, told them what had happened and begged them to come and help. "We'll pack a bag and be on our way as quickly as possible," her mother said.

They would be an hour or more so Lucille decided to go to the Manor. What she hoped for she wasn't certain, but they had all been good friends when Celia was alive and Lucille hoped to gain Anna's support and assure them that Stephen had nothing to do with his father's underhand activities.

She drove into the yard, could see lights shining from the kitchen windows. She climbed out and rushed to the door, hammering on it, feverishly. Anna opened it a fraction and peered out, "Who's there," she said with fear in her voice.

When she saw Lucille she hesitated,

" I'm not sure you should be here," she said.

"You've heard then."

"Yes, the Police rang."

"So you know Stephen's been arrested," said Lucille, with a quivering voice.

Anna could sense her emotion. She wasn't cruel.

"Come in," she said.

"He isn't guilty Anna," Lucille said, clutching her arm. "We didn't know the paintings were there. We seldom go in the loft. We've been taken in, fooled, made scapegoats, just as you have, by Elliott. He must have deliberately left them in our attic, knowing that Stephen will be locked up for hiding them on his premises. What sort of dad does that and then clears off. He probably found the paintings too valuable to deal with, so left them behind as a red herring and to give him a bit more time to get away. Anyway, when they're authenticated, you'll get them back. I'm so pleased for you. It'll be some consolation for all the other things that you have had stolen."

Anna hugged Lucille. She believed her distress was real and agreed that the return of the paintings would be more than they had hoped for.

"What will you do, now," she asked. "I'm afraid James and I will have to keep our distance. We can't be seen to fraternise with you. It might look as though we are fellow conspirators."

"I understand," said Lucille. "My parents are on their way. I'm going back with them. I can't run the farm myself. I'm going to have to dispose of all the animals. I hope Carol and Ned, my employees will help to find them new homes. I shall then be spending my time trying to prove Stephen's innocence. Dad's going to ring up his solicitor. They're on their way up here so I'd better get back and wait for them. Thank you, Anna, for listening."

They hugged, parted amicably, both worried about what lay ahead.

They were right to be worried. The big shock came several days later when the Police called Lucille, Anna and James, into the station.

Inspector Whitcombe did not beat about the bush. His face was severe when he spoke, first, to Anna and James.

"Mr. and Mrs. Sheppard, as you know six paintings were found in the loft of Mr. and Mrs. Marshall's house and we believed they were the collection that had recently been stolen from Oakdene Manor. I am sorry to tell you that they have been examined by experts who agree that they are not the genuine articles but, in fact, extremely good forgeries.

The three of them gasped.

Anna with tears in her eyes muttered, "No, I don't believe it."

James, overcome with anger shouted, "The b------, the thieving, conniving b-----. "Their hopes had been raised by the prospect of having the paintings back, but now what they would receive instead were six worthless forgeries.

It was the final blow for Anna and James and didn't take them long to work out that this canny scheme had been set up by Elliot and that his brother Douglas had been the artist involved in painting the copies. Now the police would be searching for both brothers and they hoped and prayed that they would find them.

As for Lucille her tears were of relief as Inspector Whitcombe announced that Stephen would soon be released as there was no real case against him. Being in possession of worthless forgeries was not a crime to be locked up for. Lucille said goodbye to Anna and James and hurried out to prepare for his homecoming. She knew that he would be in a desperate state and would need a great deal of help and support. She had told Anna that they would now relinquish the farm and go to live with her parents.

So, the work of the estate must go on and Anna and James would have to start looking for a new tenant for Beeches farm.

Part 5

Chapter One

Douglas stood inside the Departures entrance of Heathrow Airport with his two large suitcases and a rucksack. He was casually dressed in grey trousers, blue striped shirt and a lightweight navy jacket. For a man in his mid sixties he appeared quite fit and slim. There was no overweight stomach paunch and his greying hair, although thinning was still plentiful. He was very like his brother in that respect, except that Elliot had always been taller.

They had agreed to travel to London independently and to meet at 7 am. It was now about five past. The queue for the Check in desk was growing. In fact the whole airport was thronging with people all booking in for early flights so Douglas kept his eyes on the door, not wanting to miss Elliot's arrival.

Time passed. He'd been standing there for over half an hour. His legs were beginning to feel tired and his back ached. Where was he? Douglas hated to be late and it would take ages to get through all the security checks. They needed to get moving now, so that they didn't have to rush.

The sooner they left the country the better. Everything had gone to plan. He had copied the paintings and Elliot had kept the genuine ones and hung the replica's back at Oakdene Manor. So far nobody had noticed the switch. Elliot had also amassed a fortune pilfered from Celia's accounts and they were now going to travel to Miami, live in luxury, on their ill-gotten gains, mixing with all the celebrities for whom money was absolutely no problem and hope to buy a waterfront property, like pop stars and famous people do, along the coastline of Miami Bay.

Another half hour passed. A sudden chill ran down his back. What if Elliot didn't arrive in time. He'd tried his mobile twice. There'd been no answer. He tried it again. Still nothing. Where was he? Had he been delayed? If so he would have sent him a text. Did he intend to come? Of course he did. They'd only confirmed details a couple of days ago. Had he changed his mind? Why would he? It had all been his idea.

Douglas joined the check in queue for their designated flight. He needed to know if the tickets had actually been booked. If they had and Elliot didn't arrive he'd have to cancel them. He hoped Elliot wasn't in trouble. Why didn't he answer his phone? Perhaps he'd had an accident, or even been picked up by the police, in which case they'd be after him next. He shuddered nervously at the thought as he moved up the line.

The other scenario, that he really didn't want to believe, was that he'd been taken for a fool, that the tickets had not been booked and that Elliot had no intention of flying to Miami, or of sharing his money or his life with his brother. He couldn't believe it. They'd looked out for each other all through their lives. Why would Elliot desert him now?

Finally he reached the check in desk. The attendant asked for his passport and ticket.

"My brother has our tickets. He seems to be late. I'm wondering if I'm in the wrong queue, or whether he's booked us on a different flight."

She looked at him suspiciously.

"Name?"

"Quentin Beaumont. My brother is Winston."

Elliot had acquired passports in these names. Douglas hadn't asked how.

She checked her computer.

"I'm sorry, sir, your names are not down for this flight."

"They aren't? Really. Oh, -oh"-- his face paled as he grabbed his bags and moved away. He found a seat, still hopefully with a view of the door. He was visibly shaking and his heart was beating frantically. He knew- he was right - had to believe it. His brother had double-crossed him, used his artistic talents to his own ends, and had no intention of being with him or sharing the wealth he had accumulated.

What a fool he'd been. The brother that he had thought

he'd known all his life didn't exist. Elliot's life had been built on lies and falsehoods. He'd encouraged Douglas to create forgeries, then sell his wonderful Art Gallery and his home, and escape from the law with him, to live in another country. Now it seems, he had always planned to ditch him and disappear with it all.

He tried Elliot again. No answer.

He bought a coffee, hoping to calm himself down. He wondered how much money he had got, in his account. He had taken one out in the name of Quentin Beaumont and put all his own money into it. The sale of his Art Gallery had gone into their joint account that Elliot handled, so that was gone and all he had, basically was the money for his flat which he was still waiting for. He would check it when the bank opened.

In any case he had enough money to buy a flight somewhere. He had to leave. He wasn't safe in England any more, thanks to Elliot. Where should he go? He needed to move fast. He may have changed his name but could not alter his face so he must quit the country as soon as he could.

Immediately he thought of Spain, a place that he loved. He'd fly to Alicante, rent himself a small house by the sea, and paint. He began to relax. Suddenly the idea of being on his own, where he could live and do what he was good at and enjoyed, sounded idyllic. He could sell a few paintings, live a simple, quiet life in his few remaining years or for as long as he had before the police caught up with him. He'd grow his hair and a beard, become a bit Bohemian and hope to remain unrecognisable.

This lifestyle was far more to his taste than living the high life in Miami amongst a host of celebrities. That was all Elliot had ever wanted, to have money, attract women and mix with the rich and famous.

Purposefully Douglas picked up his cases and went in search of a flight. He was lucky. There was a seat on one to Alicante in two hours time, so after booking in his luggage he settled in a restaurant and ate a hearty breakfast. Then he got out his tablet and checked his Bank Account. The money for his flat had gone in and if he was careful he could live on that quite comfortably.

How different the day had turned out, he thought, as the plane flew over France towards Spain. He was surprised at his feelings. He was suddenly free of Elliot, the brother who had always wanted what he hadn't got and who had involved him in his wicked scams, because he could paint. The realisation that he could follow his own desires gave him a very contented feeling, as long as he wasn't recognised. He was, after all, a criminal on the run and hoped, desperately, that he would never be found.

He settled back in his seat and sipped a glass of wine bought from the trolley of a passing stewardess. He was in a window seat but all he could see were the white tops of clouds. He felt alone, but relaxed. In all honesty he'd lived under the influence of Elliot, all his life. Did that make him weak? He thought not. They had always looked out for each other from boyhood days. Not many people could admit that their mother had walked out on them and their father had committed suicide. Because of this as two teenage boys they'd naturally stuck together.

They had been privileged, given everything they wanted until their father had gambled it away. They'd gone to public school, mixed with rich and titled boys and, when they left, talked with a plum in their mouths, had all the finesse of the wealthy aristocracy, but sadly, none of the money.

Under the guidance or thumb of their uncle Percy they'd survived until they could escape. It had been Elliot's idea to ask for allowances and their uncle was quite glad to oblige and be rid of them. He had found the boys hard to handle, especially Elliot, and had his own family, with all the problems they landed on his shoulders, to contend with.

They had taken a flat together in Bristol. Douglas had supplemented their money by working in an Art shop also persuading the owner to hang some of his paintings. They started to sell. There was no doubt that he had talent. The teachers had told his parents that he ought to apply for the Royal Academy and he would have done had they been able to stay at school, but they weren't. Their father had died a bankrupt and there was no money for more school fees, so their uncle had taken them on. Douglas had always intended to paint, sell his work, earn enough money to buy his own shop or gallery and enjoy the success it brought with it. But this all took time and amassing enough money seemed almost impossible.

A smell of food wafted through the cabin and he paused in his reminiscences to order a meal, (*chicken casserole and a muffin*). His hunger satisfied he leant back and closed his eyes. Elliot's face swam before him. It was his idle nature that had been the bone of contention between them, although he had spent many years working in a garage learning all about cars, but he'd then started buying used, flashy ones, doing them up and selling them to gullible sons of the wealthy for a handsome profit.

He sat up, grim-faced, and accepted a coffee. It was because of Elliot's desire and his need that he had become susceptible to his suggestions. Elliot had started looking up some of their old school pals, the ones from titled families or those with wealthy entrepreneurs as fathers. Putting on his best public school accent he had started to meet up with some of them. This had led to invitations for hunting weekends, garden parties and visits to Ascot for the races. He'd been included in theatre trips and weekends in London, staying in town houses belonging to whichever family had invited him. Telling them a partly true story about his parents being dead and his inheritance being tied up in innumerable legal clauses, he had gained their sympathy.

His charm and easy going nature had won over the hearts of many women who were generous in their gifts and favours. Why work, Elliot had said to him, when you can live, like the wealthy, help them spend their money and promise to marry their daughters.

It was during a stay in a stately home in Herefordshire that he had come up with a brilliant idea. A pal Monty, whose inheritance this was, had started to show him round, cockily pointing out all the valuable possessions that filled each room, but it was what hung on the walls that had really caught Elliot's eye. A fortune in paintings, he'd thought as he saw the recognisable signatures on some of them.

He'd wandered around delighting his companion with his detailed study of them and in the end had selected a simple portrait that looked old and quite dark.

He'd turned to his companion and said, "You know, Monty, my brother could clean some of your grimiest paintings. This one, for instance, turning to the selected portrait. Douglas is very talented and has learnt about restoration. He'd do it for you for half the money an expensive firm would charge."

"Really, my father has always wanted to have some of the pictures cleaned and restored," Monty had said, "but the quotes he has been given made him furious. You see, Elliot, houses like this swallow money and he has to run it economically. I'm sure he'll consider your suggestion, if I ask him ---- and he did.

So the scam had begun. Paintings were given to Douglas, to clean, but instead he copied them. He became very good at it and the owners, when receiving the copy placed in the original frame, knew no different. Elliot had relied on the fact that none of these aristocrats knew anything much about Art and the genuine painting had been shipped off to the States or Europe, sold for its true value and a percentage of the sale had ended up in the Marshalls' pockets.

But after a few years the brothers had split up, due to Elliot falling for and marrying Evelyn. Because Elliot became husband and then father they'd both gone their separate and honest ways. Douglas had been glad of this, had bought a small studio and then a larger Art Gallery in Bristol and built up a good reputation as an artist, buyer and seller of works of Art.

But it had not lasted. Evelyn had sadly died and Elliot had gradually drifted back to Douglas and his old ways. He'd renewed his interest in cars, buying them cheaply and restoring them, and did this with the Land Rover that he had, this time given to Stephen for his 21st birthday.

Douglas had been glad that Elliot had eventually made peace with Stephen. A father and son should be close, not estranged and when Elliot had met Celia and told Douglas how wealthy she was, he'd been happy for him, but worried. He knew what Elliot was like and what he wanted, so he'd kept his distance from Oakdene Manor and the family. He had not wished to build up a relationship with them, because he'd guessed what Elliot intended to do --- and he'd been right. Elliot had wanted to start the painting scam again, because, in Oakdene Manor there were six valuable paintings and Douglas, fool that he was, had gone along with it.

He smiled as he realised the mistake he had made but the fact was, that, even though he had considered himself successful, he'd never had much money to spare and previously he'd been pretty good at copying paintings which, so far, had had no repercussions, so he'd relented and agreed to have another go. But now as he sat flying towards Spain he sighed because none of the money from the genuine paintings had come his way. Elliot must still be in possession of them and he Douglas, had no idea where his brother was to be found.

Chapter Two

The same day

Douglas had reasoned correctly. His brother, Elliot, was nowhere near Heathrow airport. He hadn't even travelled to London. He was, instead and at almost the same time, settling comfortably into a first class seat on a Trans Atlantic jet at Bristol airport, and would soon be crossing the Atlantic to Los Angeles, not Miami .

Elliot couldn't wait for take-off. He was very excited but also desperate to get away. He wanted to leave his sins behind him and start a new life with all the money that he'd recently acquired, --- and he wasn't travelling alone.

Beside him, elegantly relaxed, sat Sophia. To anyone watching he probably appeared as a *sugar daddy* with a glamorous bimbo in tow and in fact they would have been right. He was ageing, sadly, but still appeared an imposing figure, tall and expensively dressed in a Saville Row suit, with smoky grey eyes, a head of wavy grey hair and an essence of charm in his smile.

He had always liked to dally in bars, usually on the look-out for someone oozing money but recently the boot had been on the other foot. He was now flush, could dress with style and spend what he wanted.

On this particular night he had sauntered into a newly-opened wine bar in Bristol, flashing his diamond cuff links and had easily attracted the young, graceful, dark-haired beauty from Brazil as she sat, carefully poised, her long legs exposed elegantly. He'd assumed she was surreptitiously eyeing up prospective victims whose money she would delight in helping them to spend. That was a familiar scenario to Elliot, now *Winston* except that in all his other affairs he'd been the hunter, not the hunted.

She had deliberately caught his eye. So he was next, was he? Did he want to bother with her? He knew her type

- the female version of himself, but hey, he was rich now, entitled to a bit of fun. It would be interesting to play along and see how far she would go.

To her, his wealth had seemed obvious from his expensive watch to the well cut suit and when he'd deliberately displayed a wallet stuffed with notes she'd become as a *black widow spider* about to pounce on her prey.

He'd seen her get up to move past him and saw her stumble. She would have fallen had he not put out an arm to steady her.

"Oh,- oh. Thankyou, "she'd said shakily, in a heavily accented voice. "I-I- must have tr-ipped on these high h-eels." She'd steadied herself and looked at him. Elliot's heart had turned over. She was beautiful, absolutely beautiful.

"Can I buy you a drink, to settle your nerves?" he'd asked, helping her back onto a stool.

"Oh, thank-you, that would be lovely. Champagne, please," she'd said, smiling.

Of course, he'd thought.

He had ordered a bottle.

Things had progressed quickly. He had asked her out and taken her wherever she wanted to go, the theatre, night clubs, to dine in expensive restaurants and finally she had agreed to move with him into a suite in a 5 star hotel.

Elliot had felt a little guilty, because of Celia, although he'd known that she was frail and hadn't long to live. On several occasions he'd pleaded business dealings to Sophia, when he'd needed to visit the home before and after Celia's death and he'd also had to finish his clearance of Oakdene Manor, sort out Celia's funeral and make his final departure preparations. He'd attended the funeral but left straight after without going to the hotel for the Wake, as the next day he would be leaving the country. He knew there would be little time before he was found out and had previously discussed with Sophia where they should go next. He was desperate to get away before he was discovered.

He had obtained as much money as he could from Celia's estate, and he had, in his possession, five of the genuine paintings that had been taken out of their frames and hidden under the lining of one of his suitcases. The one of Oakdene Manor had been left in Marshall's Arts. Explaining its disappearance would have been difficult, and, after all, it was the least valuable one. He had then put the fake paintings that had been done by Douglas into the original frames, packaged them up and left them hidden at Beeches farm. He felt guilty about this but hoped they wouldn't be found too soon.

He'd been in a dilemma, had originally promised to buy tickets for himself and Douglas to fly to Miami. He'd realised, after meeting Sophia that he no longer wanted to live with his rather boring brother. He'd served his purpose creating the copies of the Oakdene Manor paintings, but now he wanted to cut him loose because he had become so enamoured with Sophia that she was the only person that mattered and the only one he wanted in his life at the moment.

They had got on well together right from the beginning. Sophia had a charming personality and when she knew him better, opened up and told him about her home and family and why she'd left. He'd been shocked at her revelation of her life of poverty with an abusive father and her need to escape from him, as soon as she could. So she'd admitted to Elliot that she'd had no choice but to use her charms and good looks to attract any man who seemed to have money to spare. She'd admitted to feeling guilty at the way she'd used them but it was her only way of existence when she realised that her looks were her greatest asset.

She had glanced at him, shyly, and he had just smiled.

"I realised the situation from the day we met," he'd said, "but having a beautiful girl to escort and spend my money on is all I ask of you."

She had thanked and kissed him and he had hoped that

she was beginning to care for him a little and became determined to make her happy.

"I really want to travel," she had told him. "I came to England because I met a man, at a reception. I was paid as a hostess. He was a property tycoon,--- built expensive London properties. He asked me to marry him. I said, yes. I wanted to get to England but when I got here I left and walked out on him. I feel bad at treating him like that. "

"Don't be" Elliot had said. " I can assure you that I've not led a blameless life myself," at which Sophia had studied his face closely but he'd given nothing away. "I decided to leave London so that he wouldn't find me and worked in clubs and bars until I ended up here in Bristol, and met you."

Elliot realised that, through him, her dream for security and wealth had begun to come true. He'd appeared cultured and affluent and she'd grown to like him and he had become deeply attached to her.

He knew, of course, that this idyllic situation would not last. He accepted what she offered, knew what she was after and she'd flattered him by being as caring as she was able whilst eagerly accepting the clothes, perfumes and exotic gifts that he showered upon her.

However, hanging over him was the problem of his brother, Douglas. Whilst he, Elliot had been living it up in a hotel with Sophia he was also supposed to have been making final preparations for Douglas and himself to travel to Miami, to make a new life.

The brothers had both known that they'd have to leave the country as soon as Celia died and Anna inherited. It wouldn't be long after that that their fraud would be discovered, so in the months before Celia's death, when her growing weakness was becoming obvious he'd persuaded Douglas to sell his gallery and flat and put the money into a joint account. He'd agreed to make the arrangements for their flight, which, of course, he did not do. However much he cared for his brother, --- and he did care, ---- they were poles apart. He had to admit that

Douglas was boring, thought only of painting and little for the opposite sex. He could not see his brother enjoying life in Miami, and, on meeting Sophia, he'd realised that travelling to the States with her was much more his cup of tea.

So he'd done the caddish thing, strung his brother along, telling him that the flight to Miami was booked from Heathrow and that he would meet him there the day after the funeral. Instead, of course he'd booked seats to Los Angeles from Bristol, for Sophia and himself. How long he would keep the Brazilian beauty interested he did not know for her greatest desire was to become a movie star, and wanted to go to Hollywood in the hope of finding fame. Elliot was no fool. He had not been taken in and knew that she would probably only stay with him until something or somebody better came along.

As for Douglas, he wished him no ill. Their relationship throughout life had been close but, as far as Elliot was concerned he did not need him anymore. He hoped he'd be alright and find somewhere abroad to live and paint, maybe Spain, a country that he knew he loved.

They had taken off. The large Trans-Atlantic jet was now thrusting its way upwards through the clouds. When it had settled at its cruising height the stewards brought round champagne. He raised his glass to Sophia and smiled.

"Here's to us and the USA," he said. She raised her glass back.

"To us, Winston," she said.

He knew exactly what she was doing, using him. Hadn't he done the same all his life, but he did not tell her that. In fact he'd told her a fabricated story about his upbringing. She believed that he had inherited an estate and sold it to live abroad. She did not know about his previous marriages or of the dreadful dealings that had caused him to change his name and leave the country. In fact he believed that she had deliberately decided not to question him. He was, to her, Winston Beaumont, a wealthy member of the aristocracy who had fallen for her beauty and had already put his hands deep into his pockets to let her follow her dream.

He smiled as he sipped his champagne. He had succeeded, had money to buy what he wanted, a villa maybe or a penthouse , a superb car and yes, what he'd always desired, --- a boat. He knew also that when or if the money ran out he had still some paintings, the genuine ones, stored safely, ready to sell.

For a blackguard he still had a conscience. This annoyed him, showing that he cared, and he knew that his conscience concerned his brother and his son. He had treated them badly. He should be ashamed, doing the dirty on his own flesh and blood like that, incriminating Stephen, with the hidden paintings, albeit the fake ones and deserting Douglas. However he was determined to look forward, forget the past, think only of himself and enjoy the moment.

This ideal scenario appeared so euphoric, and he sat back in his plush seat refusing to think of anything but the magic that lay ahead.

Yet, however easy he thought it would be to forget the past and push all his wicked deeds into the background things don't always work that way and stay hidden for eternity, and for Elliot/Winston, one sin from his past would not be lying dormant for very much longer.

Chapter Three

Back to the Prologue - 2015 continued

Anna was out shopping when her mobile rang.

"It's Carl, the foreman, Mrs. Sheppard. I'm afraid we have a problem. I think you'd better come home, immediately.------ We've found a body----"

"What was that --- what did you say?" said Anna not believing the horror that she had just heard.

"Phil, the digger driver has unearthed a body. We've stopped work and phoned the Police," said Carl.

"Oh, my god," said Anna. "I'm in town. I'll be there as soon as I can."

She hurried back to her car and rang James then set off home to Oakdene Manor. It wasn't a long drive from Cheltenham but it seemed to take forever. When she arrived her driveway was already blocked with police vehicles and, parking on the road, she ran the short distance to where a huddle of people were gathered.

Carl, seeing her, introduced her to the man in charge.

"No need Carl," she said. "Inspector Whitcombe and I are old acquaintances."

"Yes, we meet again, Mrs. Sheppard. You seem to be in trouble once more- the possessor of a body in your garden, this time," he said cynically.

They walked towards the hole made by the digger and looked down into it. A white-suited forensic officer was assessing the scene where the body, a jumbled mass of bones and scraps of fabric, lay in its earthy grave.

"What can you tell us, Chris?" asked the Inspector.

"The corpse is a female," he said, "- probably been here for about five years. Looks like she was shot through the head. I'll know more when she's moved to the lab for further investigation."

"This area is now a crime scene," the Inspector

informed Anna, "and will have to be sealed off whilst we search it thoroughly. We also need you to consider as to whose body it might be."

"We've only lived in this house for a year, as you know, Inspector, but, of course, this was my mother's home and five years ago she lived here with her second husband, Elliot Marshall. You know the rest, about his disappearance after her funeral along with much of my property and money. We're still waiting for you to find him and I wouldn't be surprised if he knows something about this, but I'm afraid I have no idea about the identity of the body."

Whilst they were standing there James arrived and after he'd looked down, shocked, into the gaping hole with its macabre occupant the Inspector suggested that they move inside for further discussion.

"It seems logical," he said, "to assume that Mr. Marshal might be involved in this, primarily because of the crime he has already committed towards you, Mrs. Sheppard, but, as yet, we have drawn a blank as to his whereabouts. Both he and his brother seem to have disappeared into thin air and Marshall's Arts is now flourishing under a different name."

"They will also have changed their names and left the country," said James, "most probably living it up somewhere exotic, on my wife's money. It almost feels as though you, the Police have done nothing. I suppose robbery comes low on your list," said James angrily.

"I can assure you that your case is still up and running, Mr. Sheppard" said the Inspector, "and certainly now that a body has been discovered we will prioritise our work accordingly. This appears to be murder and will take precedence over everything else."

"What about our building work? How long will we have to wait until the men can start again?" said James.

"What exactly are your plans?" asked the Inspector.

"We are turning the stable block into holiday cottages, so all the buildings around the yard will be under reconstruction. We are, as you know living on a knife edge, financially, and time is of the essence. We were hoping to open for business, in about six months," said Anna. "We have borrowed heavily and James is starting some consultancy work at the local hospital to keep us afloat."

"Our investigations won't take too long and I see no reason why your workmen can't continue on some of the other buildings, as long as they stay away from the investigation site."

"Oh, that's good news," said Anna. "I'll go and let Carl know."

Later, after everybody had left, James and Anna sat talking over supper. Anna suddenly realised how shaken she actually felt.

"This murder must be down to Elliot," she said.

"Of course, it's him," said James.

"It must have happened about the time that mum had her first stroke. I was so concerned about her that I never gave him much thought. He seemed plausible and caring towards mum. He proved himself to be reliable and able to keep the estate running efficiently as well as visiting her frequently. He couldn't be faulted - yet all the time he had one big master plan - to take everything for himself, We really knew nothing about him - and now this! It just shows that you can't trust anybody."

"I wonder who she is, the murdered woman," said James."If Elliot is the murderer she must be someone who found out what he was up to,- maybe imposing a threat on all his wily plans."

"The trouble is we weren't here very often," said Anna. "We've no idea who called at the house nor the sort of people he mixed with. I think the Police will have no more luck finding Elliot now than they did a year ago, nor of discovering whose body has just been unearthed."

Oakdene Manor was once more in the headlines of the

national newspapers. A murder in a country house that had already featured a huge burglary the year before, was fuel for reporters and photographers. Their presence outside the grounds was a nuisance, their reports in the papers purely speculative. They dragged up everything they could about Anna's mother and Elliot and of the theft of money and possessions that was Anna's inheritance. They snooped around, pestered for interviews and became a nightmare to the police.

Anna and James had to brazen it out. Their privacy was non- existent, their faces in all the papers caused them to be instantly recognisable and letters, phone calls, text messages, many challenging and upsetting filled them with foreboding. There were a great many offering information and the police did their best to sift through them but very few had any substance. The police were satisfied that they knew who their man was but as to identifying the body they still had no idea.

However, a few days later a car drove into the yard and Anna, standing at the kitchen window, saw a woman of about her age, climb out. She was tall, had a short, stylish haircut and wore a smart, grey suit.

Anna was surprised when she walked straight to the back door, as if she knew where she was. She waited for her to knock and wondered whether to open it. This could be another reporter with a mouth full of questions.

As she hesitated the woman knocked again and said, through the door, "Hello, Anna. I'm Marcia, your cousin. I have some information. Can I come in?"

Anna froze for a minute. A cousin - Marcia. She remembered her mother mentioning an aunt and a cousin visiting. Was this the same cousin? If so, what did she want. The alarm bells started ringing in her head. She wished James was here, but he was working,- wouldn't be home for a couple of hours.

Nervously she decided to open the door and find out more. The woman was obviously not going away.

"How may I help you?" she said.

She did not immediately ask her in but Marcia, glancing behind her whispered, "Can we speak privately? What I have to say is for your ears only."

Anna felt her heart flutter and a cold shiver ran down her spine. Whatever did this woman have to say that made her so secretive.

Looking at her intensely she decided that she didn't seem to pose any danger so she stood to one side and let her in. Anna indicated that she follow her into the lounge and they sat down facing each other.

"You may not know me Anna, but you will have known or heard of my mother, Gwenda, your father's younger sister."

"Ah, Gwenda, of course, the black sheep of the family," said Anna.

"Yes, I'm afraid so," said Marcia. "She left me with my father when I was still quite young. He wasn't good enough for her. As it turned out we were very happy together. I loved my dad and despised her. She could be very nasty and to be honest, she frightened me. I was glad that she had gone. We occasionally heard from her, but about six years ago she turned up wanting to stay. Dad was dead and I was happily married to Tony. He's in the Navy and away a lot. Tony found her money-grabbing and manipulating and didn't trust her at all. He was glad when he could escape back to sea, and warned me to be careful and try to get rid of her. He knew I had no affection for her, but she was my mother and owed her a certain loyalty. In fact she almost caused us to separate. If she hadn't disappeared again I suspect that might have happened.

I don't know whether you know, but she began to visit your mum, here. It was obvious to me why. She knew my Uncle William had died and that he'd made a lot of money and probably felt that she had the right to some of it, even though she must have known that Aunt Celia would have been the sole inheritor.

I actually came with her once and met my aunt. We got

on really well but I could sense how tense she was in mum's presence. I knew that mum was intent on causing her a lot of trouble and was so sorry to hear about her stroke. I believe that mum might have contributed to it with her constant pressure.

However, one day, quite unexpectedly, she left a note saying that she was returning to Spain, and I haven't seen or heard from her since. I was relieved but also surprised, as the days went by, that I never heard any more from her.

Seeing Oakdene Manor in the news and hearing about the mysterious body found in the grounds made me think, and the more I mulled it over, the more certain I became that the timing coincided with mum's disappearance. I'm sure that she would have continued to visit here until she'd got what she wanted and the fact that I've had no letter or phone call from her in over five years has made me question whether the body in your garden may be hers. She might have pestered Elliot once too often for money, angered him until he finally decided to kill her. Saying it like this makes it sound completely unreal, like a detective story but I've decided to go to the Police and suggest they test my DNA against that of the body. I wanted to tell you first, however, and to see if you agree that it's likely that I am right."

Anna listened intently, stunned by what she heard. It all sounded very plausible. She could see how tense Marcia was and agreed with what she proposed to do.

"I'm grateful that you came to me first, Marcia," said Anna. "Let's go into the kitchen and make a coffee. I think we both need one."

"Thankyou, I am feeling a bit queasy. It's not every day that you have to admit that your mother may have been murdered."

Anna could see her visibly shaking, and said, "I'll come with you to the Police, after we've had this drink. The sooner we know for certain, the better."

"I suppose so," said Marcia.

Chapter Four

As it was late in the afternoon Anna decided to ring the Police Station before they left to make sure that Inspector Whitcombe was available.

"Can you explain what it is that you wish to see him about?" asked the policeman at the end of the line.

"I have some new evidence about the body found at my house, Oakdene Manor," Anna replied.

"Oh, I see. Can you give me your name, please.

"Anna Sheppard and I shall be bringing my cousin, Marcia ---- "

" --- Bennett," whispered Marcia,

---"Bennett with me."

"I'll find out if the Inspector is available. Just hold the line, a minute."

It was longer than a minute but eventually he returned.

"I'm sorry to have kept you waiting, Mrs. Sheppard," the policeman said, "The Inspector is on his way back to his office and will wait there until you arrive."

"Thankyou. I'll set off shortly," she said as she put the phone down.

She decided to take her car, primarily because she knew where to go but also as Marcia was looking decidedly pale. She realised that she was facing a dreadful experience that no-one, in all honesty would wish to go through, -- the prospect of discovering that her mother had been murdered.

She settled Marcia in the car then went inside, where she couldn't be heard, to phone James. He was surprised and interested when she told him about Marcia and where they were going.

"I don't know how long we'll be," she said, "but I'll keep in touch. There's no need for you to come as well. It's not going to be easy. Marcia is looking very stressed and shaken-up."

She said goodbye then, picking up her bag and locking

the door, she hurriedly joined Marcia in the car and set off to drive to Cheltenham and the Police Station.

It wasn't a long journey, about seven miles. Marcia sat beside Anna, hardly saying a word. She shivered, as they arrived and parked. Anna could sense the alarm she felt as she opened the door for her to get out. Her body was taut, as if steeling herself for an ordeal and her eyes shone with worry.

"Come on. Let's go and get it over with," said Anna taking Marcia's arm, and walked purposefully with her into the Police station.

"Anna Sheppard and Marcia Bennett to see Inspector Whitcombe," she said to the policeman at the desk.

He looked them up and down, then at his notes in front of him. Satisfied he said, "Take a seat. I'll go and fetch him."

They sat down, close together. Anna took Marcia's hand. It was icy cold. She smiled as confidently as she could as she sat next to Marcia's still, tense profile.

They didn't have to wait long before the policeman returned and asked them to follow him. He led them along a corridor into an interview room.

"The Inspector will be with you, shortly," he said.

The room was empty except for a table with chairs on either side of it.

"This place gives me the shivers," said Marcia as she sat down. Anna agreed. It was a heartless, barren room and she could imagine all the criminal characters that had been questioned in it.

Inspector Whitcombe didn't keep them waiting long and looked curiously at Marcia when Anna introduced her.

"This is my cousin, Marcia," said Anna. " We are here about her mother, my aunt, Gwenda. She is missing, hasn't been in contact with Marcia for many years."

"Oh, really," said the Inspector, suddenly becoming interested. "Do go on."

"It's about the body that was f-f- found in Anna's garden," said Marcia, her lips quivering. "I --I have a feeling that it m-- might be her."

Anna took Marcia's hand realising that, even though Gwenda had been a trial, she was still her mother, and this whole experience was very upsetting for her.

"Just a minute," said the Inspector, and went to the door calling for some tea.

A young constable brought it in and when they were settled each with a hot cupful the Inspector asked Marcia to tell him why she thought that the body was that of her mother.

He listened keenly to what she had originally told Anna, about her mother, Gwenda's, unexpected arrival and the visits she had made to Oakdene and Celia. Also about her equally sudden departure about five years ago, that corresponded with the time that the Oakdene body had been buried.

"But why do you think anyone would want to murder her?" asked the Inspector.

Marcia dropped her head for a moment, and when she looked up, her eyes shone with tears of emotion.

"Because she was a nasty, spiteful, woman, that nobody liked, including me I'm afraid. She had never wanted me and cleared off when I was still quite young, so my father brought me up. We were very close and both of us glad that she had gone. She came back once or twice and finally landed on my doorstep about six years ago saying that she wanted to make up for all the years that she had neglected me. I realised several facts as she talked to me, that she'd had two more liaisons that were both finished and she now found herself with no house and very little money. She had come to me as I was a last resort, knew I was married with a job and a husband who was in the Merchant Navy. Her main ambition, as I later found out was to fleece my aunt Celia for some of her brother, my Uncle William's money. I honestly believe that she had been shocked at being left out of his will. She didn't seem to understand that obviously, on his death Aunt Celia would inherit everything that he had.

She was told to keep away, by Elliot after my aunt had her stroke and I thought she had. All I can think of is that she made monetary demands on him that he was not prepared to agree to and that he killed her."

"I'm very glad that you have come forward with this information, Mrs. Bennett," said the Inspector. We'll get a DNA test done. This will determine whether you are related to the body in the morgue. Also, I would like to ask you, --- and only if you feel you can, to look at the remains and the scraps of clothes that were still on it with the possibility of securing an identity.

"Oh - no - I ------," Marcia looked at Anna. "I can' -- t."

"I think you should try, Marcia," said Anna gently. "It will help the investigation."

The inspector explained that the exhumation had unearthed little more than a skeleton but there were also some bits of clothing and hair that had been clinging to it.

They were taken to the morgue. The small bundle of bones was a ghoulish sight and both women gagged and turned pale as they stared at the horror of it. Tears poured down Marcia's face as she recognised the bits of material that had been her mother's dress and the wispy hair that still clung to the fleshless head.

There was no doubt, when the results came back, that Marcia's DNA and that of the female body, matched. Even though she'd grown up without her mother and had only, some years ago come back into contact with her, finding her dead like this was a really horrifying shock.

After the test Anna invited Marcia to stay with them at the Manor for a few days. There was no way that she would let her go home by herself after this experience, especially as her husband wasn't due back from sea until the next week. Also, as cousins they had a lot to catch up on as well as being available for further police questioning.

On the way back Marcia asked about Elliot, who he was and how he'd met Celia. In telling the whole sorrowful story Anna, herself got emotional and it was Marcia who had to calm her cousin down. They stopped in a lay-by for a few minutes to give Anna time to recover.

"If only I'd trusted more on my instincts," Anna said, "maybe none of this would have happened, mum wouldn't have married Elliot and your mother wouldn't have been murdered by him. We are determined not to lose Oakdene Manor and I hope his conscience brings him down and all that money does him no good at all."

"So do I," said Marcia.

The outcome was as expected. The body was formally identified as Marcia's mother Gwenda, and the finger of guilt definitely pointed at Elliot as her murderer. The police admitted that when they had removed the body from the ground, the gun had been found beneath it obviously thrown into the hole before the corpse, and from finger prints, believed to be Elliot's, taken from the cups in the bedroom that he had been using they were able to confirm that the same prints were also on the gun. Now that they had put a name to the murdered victim a thorough hunt would begin to find the person who murdered her.

His photograph was circulated, placed in all the tabloids. His family, of course came under pressure from the press. Stephen, Lucille and all other relatives were questioned and watched. This was another blow for Stephen and when Anna spoke to Lucille over the phone she realised how the whole family were rallying round him wondering what next the police would land on their doorstep.

Also under scrutiny was the art gallery that Douglas had sold. The new owner was not pleased to find out why Douglas, the previous owner had sold it, although he admitted that he'd bought it at a bargain price. Out of goodwill he returned the painting of Oakdene Manor to Anna. Legally it was hers anyway.

However there was no evidence found as to the whereabouts of the brothers. They had told nobody what their intentions were and to all and sundry they had disappeared off the face of the earth.

Police forces across the continents were alerted, but as time passed their capture became less likely and the case was filed away awaiting new evidence.

It was in the spring of the next year that something happened that caused Anna to sit up and gasp. She was watching the news at 6 o clock whilst waiting for James to come home from work. It was the time of year for film and television award ceremonies and last night it had been the Oscars in Hollywood. The red carpet was down and many famous stars were gliding along it, stopping for photographs and interviews.

Suddenly on the far side of the carpet, his arm round the waist of a strikingly beautiful lady Anna saw the face of the man who haunted her dreams. She paused the shot and stared, then pressed the record button. James must see this. She was certain that the man she was looking at was Elliot. It must be. Nobody, surely could look so similar, his height, grey wavy hair. If only she could see more of his face. She stopped the pause and watched with concentration as the news clip continued and just as the couple were leaving the red carpet to go indoors, the man turned his head.

When she heard James open and close the back door she shrieked, "James, James! Quick! Come here! I've seen him."

"Who?" he said, hurrying in, reacting to her excitement.

"Look," and Anna showed him the recording.

"What, do you think? It's him, Isn't it?"

James stared intently at the image on the screen.

"It could be. He's very similar - hair, height, stance, and the scenario fits the bill. He'd be quite at home in the film world where there are stars, especially women or young hopefuls looking for a sponsor."

"So that's where he escaped to, Hollywood, walking along the red carpet as if he was somebody important."

"He'll just be an escort, a hanger-on," said James, "flashing his money about and attracting all the female film stars to let him enjoy their fame."

"I wonder who that dark-haired lady is that he's got his arm round."

"Some young hopeful, no doubt," said James. "Poor woman,-- if only she knew what he was like. I expect she'll drop him soon enough when someone younger comes along," he snorted viciously.

Anna was excited. What luck! They'd found their man, got him cornered.

"He mustn't be allowed to get away," she said and picked up the phone.

"We must tell Inspector Whitcombe immediately."

Chapter Five

Huge skyscrapers filled the skyline as they circled to land at Los Angeles airport. Waiting for their luggage seemed tedious but at last they were free to go. Elliot was filled with optimism as they drove in a cab towards Hollywood and the hotel he had selected the Sunset Tower Hotel on Sunset Strip. He held Sophia's hand, seeing her eyes light up as they passed along wide boulevards lined with palm trees, and saw all the people milling the streets. It was approaching dusk and everywhere was becoming alive with flashing lights and signs enticing evening visitors into shows, nightclubs and bars.

Elliot had reserved a suite, in the hotel, a temporary measure until he was able to find somewhere more permanent and, much to his delight, they were treated royally as with a flash of his diamond cuff links and Sophia's film star looks draped elegantly in *haute couture* , they were escorted in the lift to a high floor and their luxurious apartment with its huge window looking out over the city.

They couldn't believe it. They were in Hollywood, Tinsel Town, the pinnacle of their dreams, home to the movie industry and all the famous faces that went with it. Maybe one day Sophia's name would be on a star, placed in the pavement of Hollywood Boulevard. She had been desperate to come here and dreamt of being in the movies, becoming a superstar and Elliot was quite happy to help her on her way for as long as she needed him.

A year had passed and Sophia's dreams were beginning to come true. Her prospects looked good and on this particular day they were arriving at their first Oscar ceremony. Sophia had already had a few small parts in films and had been given some tickets for the Oscars by a producer who had his eye on her for several reasons apart from her acting skills. Seeing that she had an ageing money bags in tow had not seemed a problem. He knew that she would do more or less anything to be noticed and this producer could make it happen, on his own terms.

As for Elliot he was delighted to be alongside her as her escort, envied by other women and younger men. She looked beautiful, dressed in a body clinging silver dress, and many cameramen had filmed her as she walked along the red carpet.

Elliot had realised as soon as they'd arrived that cameras would be everywhere and that he was likely to get some unwelcome publicity, but ushering Sophia to the Oscar ceremony was something he did not want to miss. Thus he himself had been in on the shots, foolishly allowed his face to be caught on camera causing him afterwards to worry, knowing that the pictures would be seen all over the world and that someone from his past might possibly recognise him.

He had been desperate to accompany her and was determined to enjoy this final evening of lavish living before he had to go. Then, as soon as he could he would leave and bow out. They had had a wonderful time together and if parting from her meant keeping his freedom then that was what he had to face up to.

He had no choice. His time in Hollywood must come to an end. In a way he was glad. They had been together a year and Sophia was a huge sap on his finances.

He had rented a luxurious villa with a swimming pool, jacuzzi and a host of servants to wait on their every need. He'd found an agent for her, bought wardrobes of expensive clothes and organised the services of beauticians, hairdressers, acting and language coaches. He'd driven her about in a stylish limousine, had taken her to all the expensive restaurants, night clubs and parties that were on offer, and the result was that she had been noticed. Producers and directors had started to flock around her and although Elliot felt rather jealous when she lapped up everything and dated influential men, he had realised now that he could escape. She did not need him anymore. There were plenty of other well-minted men on the film world's stage who could satisfy her desire for fame and money and his great fortune acquired through his wily scheming, was disappearing at a very alarming rate.

He felt a little sad. Deep down he had come to love Sophia and didn't want to lose her, but he was happy that success was coming her way. She deserved a break after the awful early life she'd had to cope with in the slums of Brazil.

Elliot had absolutely adored the glitzy life of Hollywood and didn't relish starting somewhere new all over again. It was bound to be a come-down. Nowhere else, surely, could compare with this year he had spent in such a glamorous place. But he'd known it wouldn't last. There was no way he could continue spending as he had been doing. Also he wasn't getting any younger. Wouldn't attract women for much longer unless he appeared very wealthy, and sadly, after this expensive year his pockets were feeling a bit threadbare. Money, sadly does not last forever or grow, unless it is invested, but, of course, Elliot's was not.

He needed to make what he had left, multiply. *Where to go*, he wondered. Then the idea of Las Vegas came into his mind. Yes, Las Vegas, Nevada, a reasonable distance away from Hollywood. Why hadn't he thought of that before? -- a gambler's paradise. Maybe he could invest in a casino and entice people to lose all their money to him. He could sell a painting, although he was hanging onto them for emergencies. He could also play the tables. If he was lucky he would soon get back the millions of dollars that he had spent on Sophia.

He was pleased with his decision. The next morning as he showered, he decided to tell her what he intended. He didn't know how she would react. She might be glad he was leaving then she would be free to do what she liked. He hoped she would be upset and say that she would miss him.

He took her a morning cup of coffee and, as she struggled to open her eyes he sat on the side of the bed and took her hand. Their eyes met. His smiled affection, hers questioned.

She sat up and took the coffee.

"Thanks," she said. "Are you alright? You look a bit sad."

There was something melancholy about him that Sophia couldn't fathom.

"Yes, I'm fine, but I've made a decision. I hope it doesn't upset you too much but I think it's time I moved on."

" Oh!" She looked worried. "Why, --- is it me? You don't want me anymore. Have I done something wrong?"

"Oh, no, I love you dearly, but I am old and you are young. Things are beginning to happen for you and I don't want to stand in your way."

This wasn't really the truth but he wanted her to believe it.

" You need to be free to progress, Sophia. You're doing so well. I'm sure some good openings will come your way --- and you need a younger lover - not an old man like me, --- maybe a husband and family."

"But - I'm not sure I can cope - without you," she said, and her eyes filled with tears. "You are my rock. You've given me so much. How can I exist if you're not here?"

"You will, my darling. You'll be a success and when I'm in my dotage I'll follow your career knowing that I had a hand in it."

"Oh, Winston," she sobbed. "What will you do? Where will you go?"

He took her in his arms and hugged her closely.

"You know little about me, my love, and that has been deliberate on my part. I cannot tell you my plans. There are people who will come asking about me and that is the reason why I have to leave. I may have already been recognised from the recent Oscar publicity. I've made sure that you'll be alright, financially for a while. There's money in your account and the lease on this villa lasts for another four months."

"When will you go?" Her lips were quivering, as she clutched at him.

"Soon, I'll just disappear. Tell anyone who asks that I've gone away for personal reasons and will soon be back."

"And will you?"

"No, I don't think so."

"Will you ring me?"

"Of course."

He did not mean it.

When she had reluctantly and sadly left for a meeting with her agent, Elliot, now Winston, packed his bags making sure that no evidence of any sort remained to identify him. He ordered some flowers for Sophia, and then loaded up his car and drove away, dropping his mobile that he had smashed, into a bin.

Las Vegas, here we come, he thought and put the lovely Sophia and his glittering Hollywood life out of his mind.

Thus it was that he remained one step ahead of his pursuers, for already queries about him had crossed the Atlantic and soon the questions in Hollywood would begin. The Police had only to show his photo around and his false identity would be discovered. He'd warned Sophia and hoped that she would not be too upset by their investigation. She knew nothing actually about him that would help the Police except for the car that he owned. He needed to change it as soon as possible, for something else.

Time seemed to pass slowly at Oakdene Manor. Anna and James were desperate for Elliot to be caught. The Police had learnt nothing from their Hollywood enquiries. None of Elliot's friends, acquaintances nor even his lady friend knew where he'd gone.

Anna and James were incensed. They couldn't believe

that he had slipped through the net again. Where had he disappeared to this time? It was impossible to guess. He must still be in the States. He'd surely have been picked up if he'd tried to leave the country. Their only hope was that he would make a mistake, show up again and when he did the police would be waiting.

Part 6

Chapter One

Elliot didn't immediately sell his car. His vanity took over. He wanted to keep it to drive for one final time to Las Vegas so that he could enter the *Silver City* in style, ---- after which he would sell it. He knew that he had to. He could be tracked down if he kept it and anyway it was an expensive luxury and he, sadly was entering a time of frugality and needed to buy something a lot cheaper and less conspicuous.

It was a very hot journey. He was glad to roll back the roof, and drove sedately, in no hurry, letting the movement of air blow away his past life, enjoying the freedom of being once again on his own whilst he thought with delight at what he would do in Las Vegas, America's playground and the most famous gambling city in the world.

Before leaving Hollywood he'd filled the car with gas and stocked up on snacks and water. It would be a long, rather monotonous journey, about 5 hours he reckoned, along Interstate 15. Much of it would be across the hot Mojave desert so he'd need to stop a few times for a break before reaching his journey's end.

He felt very hot and tired when he eventually arrived in Las Vegas and stopped at a roadside cafe on the outskirts of town to revive himself and decide what to do next. After ordering a cheeseburger and cola he sat at a table near a window and watched as people and cars went by. It was late afternoon and the activities of passersby appeared very ordinary this far out of town. Some were shopping at grocery stores or visiting laundromats. School children hung about, laughing and fooling around on their way home and labourers from a nearby building site, having finished for the day, trudged past, smoking or chewing gum.

When he'd finished his snack he decided to drive around a bit to get his bearings. The city was even more exciting than he'd imagined and the further he got towards the centre the more lively, noisy and colourful it became. There were many really tall hotels and buildings surrounded by casinos, shops, restaurants, night clubs, all with flashing lights and signs, and, of course, hosts of people milling about, tourists hoping to make money, the wealthy in flashy cars who already had, and many more chancers on the lookout for a lucky break.

Elliot decided that the first thing to do was to find a room, not in an expensive hotel, sadly, as he had in Hollywood but one further out, so he returned the way he had come and booked into the cheapest motel he could find. The next morning he drove his car to a dealership and sold it for the best price he could negotiate. Then he took a cab round a number of used car sale rooms and picked up an economical, ordinary-looking saloon, that would be adequate for getting him about. The one thing that was obvious about the USA was that you couldn't get far without a car.

From then onwards he got up every day and travelled into town, spending his time in casinos, watching and learning. There was such a variety of games to play, Poker, Blackjack, Pontoon, Baccarat. He studied the croupiers, punters, winners and losers. He tried his luck, first on slot machines, then on the roulette tables, sometimes winning but more often losing. How did they do it, those people who walked away with enormous winnings? It didn't seem fair. The rich got richer and the strugglers got poorer. He didn't seem to realise that most people were losers in the end.

He was desperate to have an investment in a casino somewhere, but there seemed few openings for the money he had to offer, which every day got less and less as the weeks went by. He scoured newspapers for ideas, looked in Real Estate windows, shops for adverts, trolled the Internet for anyone looking for a partner to invest but there was nothing. He chatted to anyone he thought might help him but even if they were interested in someone investing he realised that he needed a small fortune which now was exactly what he had not got. If he didn't find an opening soon he would be down on his uppers looking no better than the beggars that hung around doorways.

He continued searching, day after day for any opportunity that would help him to get a foot on the ladder or become a partner but everywhere he approached he met the same brick wall, --- expense. There were hosts of people about, wanting to do exactly the same thing, all with, seemingly, a lot more money than he had. He needed a fortune to buy in with the *Big Boys* in town.

There was nothing else for it. He'd have to sell a painting. They should be worth millions, but they were unframed. He looked up prospective art dealers and experts and was prepared to travel a great distance for the chance of selling them at a good price.

He couldn't believe the outcome. Dealers were suspicious of unframed paintings even though he pretended that they had been rolled and sent by mail to him. They did not believe that they were originals, and demanded that experts be asked to check their authenticity and this he daren't let them do in case they got suspicious and informed the police, so he'd been obliged to pass them on to dubious receivers for nothing like their value just to get some desperately needed cash.

So days and months went by and his life progressed in the same heartbreaking way. He had moved from the motel to a one room apartment but had been unable to invest in any business at all. His age didn't help. He was no longer young or even middle-aged, could not rely on his looks and charm. Only by flaunting his money in swish clothes, stylish cars and generous hand outs would he ever get noticed, and this was now an impossibility. Every day he placed bets believing that his time had come, that he would hit the Jackpot. He did win, but not enough. The trouble was that every time he won spurred him on to try again. He was hooked, believed that he would win a fortune one day, but he never did.

He tried to get a job in a casino but nobody would give

one to a grey-haired man in his sixties. Anyway most of the staff were big, brawny heavies, a necessity where large sums of money changed hands.

So he cashed in everything he could, his expensive watch, rings, cuff links, flashy clothes until the day he finally sold his pathetic ordinary car and, at last, came to the inevitable conclusion that he had made a big mistake in coming to Las Vegas in the first place. Also he'd exchanged two valuable paintings for next to nothing and frittered away the money that he got for them. After arriving with such hopes he realised that he'd been a greedy fool tempted by what he thought was easy money and the outcome of it all was that in Las Vegas the only easy thing to do with money was to lose it.

One afternoon, feeling very downcast he wandered out and sat on a bench in an open area where fountains played and the flashing signs on surrounding buildings brightened up the approach of evening. People passed him by seeing just another old man whiling away the hours. He felt in his pocket and pulled out some coins. He looked at them, a few dollars and cents - enough to buy a snack perhaps.

Emotion clouded his eyes. How had he come to this? What was he to do? He'd no friends. In this place people only flocked round those with well-lined pockets. He'd made a big mistake coming here but he couldn't have stayed in Hollywood not only because he may have been found and arrested but also because his money had been swallowed up in the lavish lifestyle of keeping Sophia in comfort, and enjoying luxurious living amongst the film star community - but it had been worth it, the life of the idle rich had been all he'd hankered for, but it had also been his downfall, leaving him here, on a park bench without home, family or friends. The only family he had, and cared for were his son Stephen, and his brother Douglas, both of whom he had treated very badly. He was certain they would not want anything more to do with him.

Tears started running down his face. He was appalled. He never cried. Two men came towards him, laughing.

One carried a fistful of money. As he passed, a dollar bill fell out of his hand and fluttered towards Elliot. He bent to pick it up and give it back. As the man turned, saying, "Thanks, buddy," he saw the tears and distress on Elliot's face.

"You okay, feller?" he asked as he stopped beside him.

Elliot felt wretched, embarrassed, mortified that he had been discovered in such a state.

"Just a b-bit down on my luck," he mumbled.

"It happens to us all," the other man said.

Elliot pulled out a hanky and wiped his eyes, then stood up, ready to shuffle away.

"Here, have a bet on us," said the first man, and thrust a couple of notes into his hand. "Maybe you'll be lucky, too." He slapped him on the back and the two of them moved away.

"Thanks," said Elliot, "but I c-can't ac---- ." However the men just waved and carried on.

He did not do as they'd expected - go and fritter it away, but put it into his pocket and set off back to his lonely apartment.

This is it, he thought. *My wake-up call.*

He sat in his room, weighing up the options. He needed to leave this gambling hell that had swallowed up the last bit of money he had but where could he go? He checked up on how much money he actually had --- about fifty dollars in cash --- a pittance. He needed to be able to buy a ticket out of here. Most importantly, where could he go to feel safe? There was no point in staying in the States. He couldn't go back to Sophia and without Douglas and money his dream of living by the waterside in Miami was well and truly over. Should he return to England? Would they be watching for him at the airports? If he did manage to get there where could he go? He couldn't go anywhere near Oakdene Manor. Anna and James would immediately call the Police and what if the body of that dreadful woman had been found and they suspected him, he'd be arrested for murder.

He wondered what had happened to Stephen. He'd probably wrecked the poor boy's life. Stephen would have been a good hard working, hopefully prosperous farmer by now if he, Elliot hadn't turned up. He felt bad. He'd set his own son up by planting the forgeries, to cover his own tracks. Had Stephen been tried, imprisoned? If so the guilt lay heavily on Elliot's shoulders and he knew he wouldn't be welcomed if he sought him out.

Then there was Douglas, his brother who he had grown up with, used his skills and then stole his money, destroyed his livelihood, and abandoned him. What sort of a person treated someone so close to him like that? Suddenly in his dotage he was becoming considerate and caring. Where had all this deviousness, theft, swindling and murder got him? Nowhere. He was a lonely man with little money, soon to be homeless with no-one in the world who loved or cared for him.

What did he really want to do? He thought long and hard. Douglas kept entering his mind. They'd been together for a lifetime. Clung to each other when left orphaned. He would go and find him, apologise and try to make amends. Would Douglas have him back? Would he help him? Douglas wasn't a mean man. Elliot had always thought him a little weak, actually, probably because he was one-track minded where Art was concerned. He'd no real ambition, not like me, Elliot thought. Surely, if I find him, he'll forgive me, --- and feeling more positive, he started to plan his departure.

Chapter Two

A few days later

Elliot had made up his mind and he felt happy with his decision. He'd sold the last of the paintings, again at a knock down price, but at least he had a bit of money in his pocket for the journey. He then bought a one-way ticket to Alicante via Heathrow under a new name, Thomas Hughes. He'd three passports altogether. He'd used two of them so he now adopted the third and changed his appearance accordingly.

To look like Thomas Hughes he had to have his hair cut short and sport a pair of dark glasses. He also stopped shaving, allowing a stubbly beard to grow, and bought a baseball cap to wear. Looking and feeling like a new person he travelled to the airport muttering rather sorrowfully, "*Goodbye USA*" as he passed by all the glitzy temptations that had stimulated his longing yet had caused his downfall.

It had been wonderful, to begin with when he had lived with Sophia, but then sadly his past had caught up with him and he'd left her to try his luck in Las Vegas which had turned out to be a disaster, so now escape was all that he could do. Would he always be looking over his shoulder and keeping one step ahead of the police? He hoped not. Perhaps in Spain he could disappear, find Douglas and live out his life in peaceful anonymity.

It was a long journey across the Atlantic and when he landed in England he was terrified that he would be recognised,--- but he wasn't. A different name and camouflaged look did the trick but it didn't stop him waiting nervously in the Departures area at Heathrow until he was able to climb aboard the flight to Alicante. When they finally took off he knew that he was on the last lap, a couple of hours away from his destination.

He was wonderfully relaxed as he walked out of the airport, and as he travelled towards Javea, felt free and safe. He couldn't wait to see Douglas. He was pretty sure he knew where to find him, --- somewhere on the waterfront, painting. They had often come here for holidays, when Douglas would settle to paint and he - well he'd always been on the outlook for opportunities. He couldn't wait to surprise his brother. He was an eternal optimist, would beg his forgiveness. He believed that Douglas wasn't the sort to bear a grudge for long. He'd probably be glad that he'd come to find him. They could then settle, together, to a comfortable retirement in the warmth and tranquillity of Spain.

On arrival, he looked for somewhere to stay. He didn't expect it would be for very long, so certain was he of finding his brother. He eventually chose a small guest house, near the harbour. His room was cosy and quaint but he only wanted it to be temporary. His landlady, Rosina, was a widow and curious to know his reasons for staying. He told her a mostly true story about his search for his brother, and the hope that he would soon find him as he couldn't afford to stay for long without earning some money.

Rosina, felt sorry for him and offered him a reduction for his room if he did some jobs for her.

"I am a lonely widow," she said, tearfully, in her stuttering English and have no man to work for me."

Alarm bells began to ring in his head and Elliot knew he would have to be careful. Getting mixed up with a buxom senora was not what he wanted. He was beginning to feel his age and she looked as if she could be very demanding, but her offer was based on good intentions so he agreed to do some obvious maintenance on the old building saying that when he wasn't working he would be searching for his brother.

After he'd settled in he was desperate to start his search so he walked along the waterfront of Javea but was disappointed that he saw no sign of Douglas or even any artists at all. So day after day he started to travel from Javea along and through all the small coastal settlements. He wandered along the seafronts, looking in shops especially ones selling paintings. He had an old photograph of Douglas that he showed to people in eating places, boatmen in harbours or locals about their day to day business but it didn't prove very helpful as it was rather out of date.

As the days passed he became more and more downcast. He helped Rosina but did not open up to her. She surprisingly didn't push him, was aware of his longing to find his brother and realised how miserable he was becoming.

He knew that he daren't go to the authorities. They would ask too many questions so he spent his time staring hard at strangers hoping for some recognition - and one day it happened, in reverse, without his knowing - someone saw and recognised him.

Douglas was on his way to meet up with a couple of pals for a drink. It was a hot day. The sea front, at Javea, Avenida del Mediterraneo was busy as usual with tourists sauntering about. Suddenly a slight disturbance caught his eye. A man was accosting people, and handing out leaflets. Most of them were dumped in a bin after he'd passed. Something about the man's stance, height and white hair triggered a memory, an unpleasant memory.

Surely not, thought Douglas, feeling a cold shiver run down his spine. *It's not him. It can't be.* The man moved on and Douglas sidled up to one of the bins and, without drawing attention to himself, picked out one of the crumpled pieces of paper.

He paled when he saw his own face, albeit years younger, smiling from it.

He dived into a shop, peered out of the window and studied the figure of - yes, his brother. There was no doubt in his mind. It was Elliot walking along, stopping frequently to question people and show them the photograph.

Forgetting his rendezvous with his friends he left the shop, pulled his hat well down as if to shield his head from the sun and hurried back home.

It wasn't far. He lived in a small house near the harbour with a balcony overlooking the sea where he often sat to paint. Today, however, he collapsed into an old comfy chair set in the afternoon shade and looked around at the familiar scene, but he did not see it, so shaken was he from the horror of almost meeting his treacherous brother again.

Time had passed for Douglas. He had got over the shock of being left at the airport. He'd come to the place he loved best and settled down. With the money that he had managed to keep from Elliot he had bought his house and decided to spend the rest of his life painting. He earned some money helping in a local bar, where he exhibited some of his paintings and a few tourist shops also hung some of his work and he was able to make enough to live the simple life that he so adored.

He now spoke Spanish well, had made many friends and had practically pushed his past life into the background. He had no desire to have any more to do with his double-crossing brother.

But fate obviously was not going to allow this to happen. His nemesis had appeared to upset his comfortable retirement. Elliot! Elliot! His very name was enough to make him throw up. *What was he to do? Would Elliot find him? Did he want to be found? NO- no, absolutely not.*

He phoned his friends, pretended to be feeling ill, then remained, in his chair, as the sun set and darkness crept in. His mind would not let him rest, questioning why Elliot was looking for him. He should be rich, living it up on all the money that he had stolen. *Where had he gone instead of meeting him at the airport?* There was only one thing that his brother had ever desired, money - and lots of it, and it was obvious, now, to Douglas that he was on his uppers, had somehow wasted a fortune and he was looking him up as a last resort, probably hoping that he, his brother, had still got some that he could spend.

Well he wouldn't get it, not a chance, Douglas thought and determined to lie low for a few days allowing Elliot to move on. In any case he had little money to spare. He'd only enough to enjoy this tranquil existence that he had found for himself. His brotherly love had disappeared on that fateful day that he was left stranded at the airport, and Douglas could and would not forgive him.

He moved, at last, from his chair, felt his stomach rumble. He'd go down to the local bistro and buy a bite to eat. He looked in the mirror. The younger Douglas was not really recognisable. He was now almost white, rarely shaved and his skin had darkened in the sun. His shirt and trousers were well worn and comfortable and when he pulled his hat firmly on his head no-one in the street would ever give him a second glance.

The next couple of days were torturous. Douglas couldn't get Elliot out of his mind. He didn't want to see him or help him but also he couldn't bear the thought of his having fallen on hard times. Elliot obviously wanted to find him and in the end, Douglas could not, in all honesty, shrug his shoulders and ignore the situation.

He rifled through his pockets and pulled out the crumpled flier. An address was printed on it, *Villa Reposa, Avenida Carlos, Javea.* He located it on his phone and with a heavy heart set off to find the house where his brother was staying. He stood outside for many minutes trying to settle himself and also wondering what he was going to say when he came face to face with the one person he really did not want to meet.

Finally he crossed the road and knocked on the door. An attractive lady of middle age answered.

"Buenos dias, senora," he said. "I believe my brother is staying here."

"Your brother, senor," she said. "What is his name?"

"Elliot - Winston --- " Douglas realised that he had no idea what name his brother was using.

The senora looked at him closely then gasped --- "You're Tomaso's brother, aren't you?

"Tomaso - ah, does he look a bit like me?" Douglas asked.

"Si-si", she said. "He came to find you -- but he go, about an hour ago. You are too late."

Douglas initially felt relieved at this news but afterwards realised that he was curious as to why his brother had come looking for him.

"Do you know where he's gone?"

"He did not say. He was a lovely man - helped me do jobs. I'm on my own you see - no man to help me."

Douglas stepped backwards. Her eyes looked him up and down and he sensed her need. He couldn't wait to get away but he wondered why Elliot had wanted to.

Here was a lonely woman with her own business. Just the meal ticket Elliot thrived on, but he hadn't stayed. *Why?* Perhaps he really was past it. Wanted to spend his last years with him, instead of in the demanding arms of a buxom Spanish lady.

He said, "Adios, senora" and turned to leave. He might as well go home. There was nothing more he could do. He'd missed Elliot. He'd been too slow in his decision to contact him. Part of him was sorry but the other part was, in fact, highly relieved. Elliot was trouble and he did not need him. Selfishly, or was it, he decided to put him out of his mind and return to the happy life that he had created for himself.

But his conscience wouldn't let him. Instead of returning home he wandered about, studying people, just as Elliot had done, in case he spotted where he had gone. He knew he was a fool at even considering to meet him again, but Douglas was not an unfeeling man. He had a heart, and cared.

Elliot, however, seemed to have disappeared. *Where would he go?* thought Douglas. He's probably heading for the main road out of here. He found himself hurrying, leaving the sea behind and going in search of the road travelling North.

After a while he began to tire. It was hot and he'd

brought no water. He perched on a shady wall and wondered how much longer to carry on. The road was busy. There was a lot of traffic leaving Javea. A lorry passed by and he saw someone ahead flag it down. Was that Elliot? He got up quickly and rushed towards him, shouting, "Elliot! Elliot! Stop - wait," but he was too late. Elliot hadn't heard him. His voice was drowned by the noise of engines and by the time Douglas was half way there he had climbed aboard and the lorry had moved on.

Oh, no!" cried Douglas, dropping his head in his hands. "I'm too late. I've missed him."

Chapter Three

Elliot was not in a good place. He felt very despondent. He'd been in Javea for several weeks and had been true to his word helping Rosina. He'd cleaned gutters, mended faulty window catches, tidied her outhouse and pruned some of the sprawling bougainvillea. Her list of jobs was endless but he got up early and worked until it became exhaustingly hot. Then he would have a quick lunch and spend the rest of the day travelling up and down the coast, wandering the streets and waterfronts, showing people the picture of Douglas and finally collapsing in the shade when he felt exhausted. But even then, his eyes did not rest. He still watched people as they passed by, searching their faces for possible recognition but he was always unlucky. It seemed as if his brother was nowhere to be found.

He knew he couldn't stay at *Villa Reposa* for much longer. His money had almost run out. Finally he told Rosina that his search had failed, that there wasn't any point in him staying. He couldn't afford to pay for a room even at a reduced rate, and that he would be moving on the next day. She was upset and sorry to see him go but even the offer of work and free accommodation would not change his mind. He knew that if he stayed he would succumb to her amorous advances and in his younger days he would certainly have taken advantage of what she was offering him. He knew that he could have settled down with her, but to be honest he didn't want to, hadn't the energy to take up with another woman nor the desire to end his days in a small seaside guest house, working as an odd job man.

"Where will you go?" Rosina asked tearfully as she packed him a bag full of food to help him on his way. "I will miss you."

"I'm not sure. I haven't been able to find my brother. Maybe I will be luckier in looking for my son," he said.

Not wanting to prolong his departure he kissed Rosina on both cheeks, thanked her for her hospitality and picking up his bag walked away, down to the sea. He sat on a wall, looking out at the gently rolling waves, at the fishing boats in the harbour, and all the happy holidaymakers sauntering along.

Desperation welled up inside him. He could have stayed in this lovely environment, worked for Rosina. They probably would have settled down to a comfortable relationship and the balmy weather really suited him, but inside there was this terrible longing to make amends with his family. He had failed to find Douglas, had felt certain that he would be here in Spain, but he wasn't, and if not here where would he have gone? The obvious answer was -anywhere, in which case Elliot knew he had no chance of finding him.

It had crossed his mind, in the last few days that Douglas was, in fact, here in Javea, had seen but deliberately avoided him. Elliot's ego, always having been his downfall, could and would not believe that, having seen him, Douglas would have decided not to make contact.

Anyway, he'd been here for several weeks and had not the money to remain any longer. He would have to take up his other option, to go back to England, find his way to Bristol, and try to find Stephen.

He couldn't travel by air. He'd only bought a one way ticket, so sure had he been that he would find Douglas and be re-united. Now he hadn't enough money to buy another so he'd have to thumb for lifts through Spain and France until he reached the Channel. It would be hard and he'd no idea how long it would take. He was completely in the hands of anyone who was good enough to offer him a lift. Would he make it? He knew that age and the length of the journey were against him.

Finally he moved from the sea wall and made his way to the main road. He was lucky enough to get a lift in a lorry to Valencia. He did not see the frantic waving of a figure at the side of the road. If he had, his troubles would have been over and he would have been reconciled with his brother, but fate had decided otherwise, leaving the two people, blood relations, upset and full of remorse as they missed each other by the narrowest of margins.

Whilst Elliot made his sorrowful journey to Valencia, Douglas wandered back home, knowing that he would now not have a moment's peace because he had failed to meet up and help his brother who obviously had need of him.

In the lorry Elliot found that the lorry driver, Pedro was glad to have someone to talk to but was rather surprised that his companion wanted to reach Calais.

"It's over a thousand kilometres, senor. Why not go by train?"

"No money," Elliot replied. "I've let a fortune slip through my fingers," and he turned his head sideways so that the driver couldn't see the tears that welled up in his eyes.

Pedro was a kind, sympathetic man, sensed the desperation that showed on Elliot's face and thrust a few Euros into his hand when he dropped him off at the truck station in Valencia.

"Gracias," Elliot said, "but I can't ---." He was too late. Pedro had already driven off.

Not all drivers were so pleasant and generous. Very few actually offered him a lift, so he walked, more than he rode. The food that Rosina had given him lasted a few days. He headed north stopped in villages, asking for work. He was prepared to do anything for a few crusts of bread. He was lucky enough to be able to join in with the grape harvest, picking until his fingers turned purple and helped to load barrels of wine onto carts. Mainly he looked for garages and asked for work. He was successful once, in a small town and was also able to rent a room. He started feeling comfortable again and almost decided to stay, but he didn't.

So once more he took off on his lonely trek determined

to complete his journey and see his son once more. Day followed day. Sometimes he got a lift, crossed the border at La Junquera in the back of a cart full of vegetables, then used his last few Euros to travel by bus across part of the Pyrenees, to avoid the climbs and the cold. After that it was just a long daily trudge. He didn't know where he was going. He tried to stay on the main roads where there was the likelihood of a lift and headed for towns hoping to find food and shelter. Places like Lyon and Dijon appeared on signposts but how much further he had to go he had no idea.

The further he walked the more tired he got. His bag weighed heavily on his scrawny shoulders so gradually as his clothes became foul and dirty he threw them away. He was forced to sit in busy subways, stations or shopping areas, begging, until he was moved on. With the little money he gained he bought food. Often he resorted to theft of bread or fruit from stalls and counters, or rifled through rubbish bins outside cafes.

He was becoming dirtier as each day passed. He splashed a bit of water on himself in public toilets and slept in doorways or anywhere that might offer shelter.

His progress through France was extremely slow and his health suffered from exposure and hunger. Drivers no longer offered him rides. His appearance put them off. He began to hallucinate. Dreams and images of his past life buzzed in his head. The weather got colder and he developed a hacking cough and shaking limbs until he could hardly put one foot in front of another. He had no warm clothes so snuggled in corners and doorways wrapped in old plastic bags.

One day, in a car park he found a van unlocked and stole a coat, gloves and a half nibbled sandwich. The coat was wonderfully warm and he gave no thought to the poor man who, when he returned, would curse himself at the discovery that he had been robbed because he had not locked his van.

So Elliot struggled on. From the road signs it seemed that he was not getting any closer to Calais? He didn't realise that his progression was less each time he set off because his energy and stamina levels were at a very low ebb. He had become so weak that he could hardly stumble to his feet each morning and inevitably the time came when he knew that he could go no further. In utter misery he collapsed in a doorway, unable to move, his confused and sickened mind not realising that he was finished and about to die.

But even death was not ready to receive him. Only Elliot could have chosen the one door that would lead him to a safe sanctuary. Early in the morning it was opened by Sister Lucia, one of the Sisters of Mercy, whose mother house this was, on the outskirts of Calais. She immediately called for help and Elliot found himself being held on either side as he tottered along a corridor and placed carefully on a narrow bed. He opened his eyes, saw the white-robed, smiling face of Sister Lucia and thought he'd arrived in heaven.

"I've made it," he muttered as they removed his soiled clothes and bathed his aching body. From then onwards he knew nothing until one morning daylight forced his eyes open. He turned his head and saw a nun sitting beside his bed. His movement disturbed her from the book she was reading and she got up and called with excitement, "Sister, sister, he is awake."

From then onwards he started to improve. The kindness of the nuns was beyond belief and, in his weakened state his eyes were constantly full of tears and his heart full of gratitude.

His recovery was slow. He was old and very weak. They fed him with soup, dressed him in clothes that hung limply on his emaciated body and helped him to walk and gain strength in his legs. He spent his time watching the nuns living their lives in this peaceful setting and often stumbled along to their small chapel to pray for forgiveness from all the people that he'd treated badly throughout his life. He even remembered Gwenda but with horror wondered how the nuns would react if they knew that they were helping to heal a murderer?

But he would not completely recover. When the doctor felt he was strong enough he told him that he'd had pneumonia and pleurisy, that his lungs were damaged and he would never regain all his strength.

They asked him about his family, worried that he had nowhere to go. He told them a little, that he'd been travelling to find his long lost son who he said would welcome him, but they did not totally believe him.

"We can find you somewhere here to live and some work," said the Mother Prioress. "You are not strong enough to travel far." So he stayed a little longer, willingly helped in the garden but realised how little he could do as a little bit of exertion completely exhausted him.

One day he said to them, "I cannot stay any longer. "Soon I will be too weak to travel and I must -- go home --- find my son"

They knew that he was determined, so bought him a ferry ticket, dressed him warmly, gave him some food and a little money.

"Adieu," they said. "Bon Voyage."

He held their hands and thanked them for nursing, caring and saving his life. Never had he met such kindness. They had been his salvation and he knew it, and for a while as he set off for the ferry, he felt very lonely realising that once again he was on his own.

Chapter Four

A week later - Oakdene Manor

Anna was watching a grey squirrel darting across the lawn. There were so many of them about and they were becoming a nuisance in the garden. As she turned away from the lounge window she heard a knock. She went through the hall to the kitchen and saw Sally Cook, wife of the new tenant of Beeches farm standing outside the back door, holding a letter.

" -- 'Morning, Anna," she said. " Sorry to disturb you but this came in the post, for Stephen Marshall. Usually I re-address any letters, not that there are many, now, but this is from Spain, so I brought it to show you first."

Anna took the letter, noticed the stamps and the writing. It was not a hand that she recognised.

"Oh, thanks, Sally," she said. "I'll see what it is and post it on to Mr. Marshall."

She knew that Sally was curious but did not open the letter in front of her or discuss who it might be from. As she closed the door she studied the envelope. The address said,-

Mr. Stephen Marshall
Beeches Farm
Westford
Nr. Cheltenham
Glos.
England.

It had been stamped about five days ago in Javea, Spain.

The past reared its ugly head as she looked at it and her heart started beating as she wondered who had sent it. The writer obviously didn't know that Stephen and Lucille no longer lived at Beeches Farm. *Could it be from Elliot*, she wondered as curiosity gripped her. She was desperate to open it but knew she must not.

Instead she rang Lucille.

"Anna --- how nice. How are you?" came Lucille's voice at the other end of the phone.

"I'm fine," Anna replied. Lucille must have sensed a certain excitement in her voice.

"Is everything alright?" she asked.

"Well, I'm not sure. --- Sally, you know, the wife of Ian who took over Beeches - your farm, has just come with a letter for Stephen."

"Why didn't she redirect it like she usually does?" asked Lucille.

"Well, because it's come from Spain. Everyone in the village knows that we originally thought Elliot and his brother had disappeared there. I'm glad she brought it to me and didn't send it straight on to you or Stephen might have opened it first. I'm wondering if I should see who sent it, Lucille, and read it to you. Then we'll both know what it's about and whether we should show it to him.

"Go on then, Anna. Open it. I'm dying to know who it's from."

Lucille heard a rustle of paper, down the phone. Then a gasp.

"What is it? Who's written it?"

"Douglas -- Douglas Marshall, Elliot's brother."

"Really! Go on, Anna. Read it," said Lucille excitedly.

16 Avenida de Abona
Javea
Spain

Dear Stephen, she read.

I'm sure I'm almost the last person that you wish to hear from, and in writing to you I realise I may possibly be putting my head in a noose, but I feel compelled to do so. My reason is to warn you that your father is on his way to you.

I have an idea that you are his last resort, especially as he could not find me.

"That's strange," interrupted Lucille. " I thought that Elliot and Douglas had run away together."
"Apparently not," said Anna.

I have, all my life, gone along with your father's criminal ideas and shamefully admit to creating reproductions of the six paintings from Oakdene Manor. However, I became a victim too. We had planned to fly to Miami, the day after his wife, Celia's funeral, but I waited at Heathrow airport for him and he did not arrive. I discovered that he had not booked any tickets for us and obviously had no intentions of spending the rest of his life with me. He had pocketed all the money that he had stolen, even from the sale of my Art Gallery and I was left with only the money from the sale of my flat, which had been delayed.

I was so shocked, mad at myself for trusting him and when I started to think what to do next I decided to fly to Spain, a country that I love, and settle down to live a life that suited me far more than the American dream would have done.

"Well," said Anna. " So Elliot double-crossed his brother."
"Something must have happened to make Douglas break cover," said Lucille. "Go on, Anna."

But, a few weeks ago, I had an unwelcome surprise. The brother that I had never wanted to see again, or expected to, turned up in Javea. I saw him handing out papers to people on the seafront, and when I pulled one out of a bin, that had been thrown away I saw a picture of myself, very much younger looking, thankfully. I knew then that he was there to find me.

But I didn't want to be found. He would not have easily recognised me as I've grown my hair and dress more casually. I'm afraid I hid from him, whilst I decided what to do. I couldn't believe how he'd changed. He looked old and hard-up, certainly not the flush, sassy man that I expected him to be. I got the feeling that he's lost all the fortune that he took from Anna and it seemed obvious that he's penniless once more. I think he had come searching for me as a last resort to spend anything that I had left.

"Oh, Anna, I'm so sorry," said Lucille. "Your fortune -- -- all gone."
"Don't worry, Lucille. We're surviving. I never really expected to get anything back. I'm beginning to feel for Douglas, though. It seems that he's been used, too." She read on

I deliberately kept a low profile. My friends thought I was recovering from an illness, but in reality I was staying away from where he might be. From then on, of course , I couldn't get him out of my mind and knew that I would have no peace until I faced him and found out what had happened and what he wanted, so I fished the paper with my picture on, that I'd pushed crumpled up into my pocket and found the contact address that was printed on it. He had obviously been staying in a guest house by the seafront but by the time I finally decided to call on him I found that he had left a short time before. I hurried after him but I was too late. I saw him flag down a lorry, climb into the passenger seat and drive away. I waved and shouted frantically but he did not see or hear me.

I knew where he intended to go because the lady in the guest house told me that he had decided to return to England to find his son.

As to when he does find you, Stephen, if he is able, I do not know. He did not look good. His clothes were shabby and he appeared thin and undernourished.

I am writing this to sort of appease my conscience but

whether I will ever get over turning my back on my brother, as he did to me, is a question that I cannot answer.

I wish you and your wife well and hope that, if Elliot does arrive on your doorstep you will do what you feel you must. He has not been a good father to you and you have every right to hand him over to the Police. If this brings the law down on my head too - I will not blame you.

Your uncle

Douglas

Anna heard a sniffle at the end of the phone.

"Are you alright, Lucille?"

"I was just thinking what a frank and melancholy letter it is," she said as she blew her nose.

"What are you going to do?" asked Anna.

" Well you'd better send the letter here and I'll have to show it to Stephen. He'll need to be prepared. Elliot might turn up any day, although I'm not sure he knows that we no longer live at Beeches Farm, so he might come to you first."

"Do you want me to give him your address?"

"You'll have to, won't you."

"I suppose so, but it sounds as though he's not fit enough to cause much trouble. In any case I'm sure we all hope that Stephen decides to hand him over to the Police."

"I'm sure he will. I think I'll write to Uncle Douglas unless Stephen wants to.

He's been honest and straightforward with us, but it's up to you, Anna, if you want to press charges against him."

"I know."

Anna posted the letter on and a few days later Lucille rang to say that she was going to write to Douglas on Stephen's behalf. She said that Stephen was adamant about giving his father up to the Police, if and when he turns up.

His reaction to Douglas was surprising.

"He hardly knows him, Anna, and wants me to say that he will not tell the Police where to find him."

"That's very generous of him," said Anna. "However I don't think I can feel the same. After all he did copy my dad's paintings and I'm pretty certain that we will never get the originals back. However what's done is done and we have survived, so I'll honour Stephen's decision."

Douglas was pleased and surprised to receive a letter from Lucille. He sat on his balcony feeling slightly nervous about what she had written and knew, at any moment that the officers of the law might come and arrest him.

"Dear Uncle Douglas,

I am writing this on Stephen's behalf. He feels he cannot write to you himself. He has suffered mentally due to the way his father treated him. We decided to give up the tenancy at Beeches. He couldn't bear to live and work there any more so we now live with my family. My father runs a stud farm and I work for him. Stephen helps with the books etc.

The way Elliot treated us was abominable. We were so happy before he arrived. Stephen had taken over the farm, on the Oakdene estate and had begun to work hard trying to make it pay. I started up a riding school, with Celia's help and then she met your brother. You know the rest but what you probably don't know is that Elliot deliberately tried to implicate us. He parcelled up the replica paintings and hid them in our loft at Beeches farm.

Douglas gasped.

The police, of course, came to question us and found the paintings when they searched the house. We were horrified. Elliot must have planted them on us to throw suspicion our way thus giving himself a bit more time to escape.

Stephen was arrested but released when it was discovered that the paintings were replicas. He was shattered and had a nervous breakdown from which I'm afraid he will never properly recover.

As you can see there is no way that Elliot will be welcome here. Fortunately he does not know where to find us so will have to go to Beeches Farm or Oakdene Manor where the present occupiers of Beeches, and Anna and James will be waiting for him.

What you may also not know is that Elliot is also wanted for murder---

Douglas stiffened. Murder -- no - - surely not.

--- the murder of Anna's aunt, Gwenda. She had been visiting Celia just before her stroke and probably afterwards, too. She must have found out what your brother was doing and challenged him. Her body was discovered buried in the grounds of Oakdene Manor. It had probably been there for about five years and only discovered when the ground was dug up for alterations to the stable blocks, a couple of years ago. The Police have proved that Elliot is the murderer. They found the gun with his fingerprints on, buried beneath her.

"Oh, my God," said Douglas, throwing the letter down. He stood up and paced the balcony. His face was grim. Elliot, his brother was a murderer.

"How could he," he moaned, --- "be so wicked?

After a few minutes he calmed down enough to pick up the letter and read to the end.

If you didn't know about this it will come as an awful shock, but your guilt at not letting him contact you, recently, might change to relief that in doing so you have had a lucky escape. Who knows what else he may have drawn you into.

As yet Elliot hasn't arrived here.

We will keep you informed if and when he does and Stephen has agreed that your whereabouts in Spain will remain a secret.

Your niece
Lucille

Douglas breathed a sigh of relief. This was the end. He was finished with Elliot, --- no longer wanted to call him *brother*. He was so thankful that he had not met up with him, and could now carry on with his painting and relaxed life style in this idyllic corner of Spain. He was also full of gratitude to his family, knowing that they would not hand him over to the Police. They had realised that he had been a victim, too, entwined in the spider's web of a wicked schemer.

Of course Douglas was aware that if Elliot did get arrested he would probably give him away and Stephen and Lucille might not feel they could lie to them about his whereabouts. He would not blame them but at the moment Elliot had not shown up at Beeches farm and he hoped it would be a long time before he did. It seemed obvious that something must have happened to him because he should have been there by now, --- so where had he got to?

Chapter Five

It was raining when Elliot boarded the ferry and as the wind whipped up the sea it made the crossing a challenge. He found a seat inside where he stayed for the whole journey watching the wintry sea through the windows as it tossed the boat with unrelenting power and splashed the glass with a froth of white spume. Luckily he did not succumb to *mal de mer* like many other passengers. Instead he enjoyed the warmth and comfort of the ship, knowing that once he disembarked he would have to decide where to go, and how to use the little bit of money wisely, that the nuns had given him.

His main purpose was to reach the West Country in the hope of finding Stephen although he wasn't sure where to look. Would he still be working on his farm? If not maybe he was living with Evelyn or Lucille's families. His other thought that made him feel ashamed was that he might be in prison. He hoped he wasn't. He felt very guilty about what he had done, hiding the paintings in the loft of Beeches farm, where they would easily be found. On his part it had been a red herring, a desperate attempt to transfer the search by the police away from himself. He'd hoped that Stephen, if put in custody would have soon be released when they discovered that the paintings were not genuine.

He knew that he would most likely not want to see him or have anything to do with him. How can a son whose father had treated him so badly, ever want or trust him again? He would have to beg forgiveness, when he found him, let him see how he was suffering, mentally and physically, that he wanted to make peace with him before he died which was, in fact, the truth.

They would all see that his circumstances had altered, that he was no longer wealthy, but poverty stricken, destitute and with bad health. How would Stephen and Lucille react to that? Laugh at him -- be pleased that he was suffering. If so, he knew that he deserved it, but, even so, he had to find Stephen. He was all he had left.

Elliot's weakness would not allow him to walk far so he had to rely on lifts. From Dover he hitched a ride in a lorry carrying vegetables to London and was dropped off near Covent Garden. He hung around for a few days enjoying being in the capital and joined the ranks of the homeless queuing at soup kitchens.

His journey west was slow. He travelled wherever a driver took him. Just being offered a lift was all that he sought. Being in the warm, not having to walk and often sharing the driver's food helped him to survive. Over a period of a week he went to Portsmouth, Windsor, Oxford, Sheffield, Rugby and eventually Bristol.

Standing in the heart of the city he tried to decide how he was going to contact Stephen. He needed a phone so that he could ring or text him. Everyone who passed him by had their eyes glued to phones. He remembered Stephen's number at Beeches Farm but there were few public phones about these days. He couldn't walk into a police station for help. They'd ask his name. It would be like stepping into a lion's den with no way out. Perhaps he could steal a phone, but how? People often put them down on tables or counters but he'd have to be quick to nab one and speed was one thing that he was not good at any more.

The best thing he could do would be to find his way to Oakdene Manor. It was a fair distance, via Gloucester and Cheltenham and his money that he could have spent on a bus, had long gone. He wondered if Anna and James would still be there, whether they had been forced to sell because he had left them penniless. He had never felt guilty about that. Why shouldn't he have had Celia's money. He'd been her husband --- had rights.

If they were still there, they'd know what had happened to Stephen, whether he was still at Beeches Farm or moved away. He knew that he wouldn't be welcome, but they surely wouldn't turn a poor, sick old man away, would they? He needed his family to forgive him and look after him, give him a home where he could live out his final years.

Only Elliot in his weakened state could imagine this happy ending, that, in all honesty, was never going to happen especially as he seemed to have totally forgotten that he was a murderer, although he had no knowledge that the body of Gwenda had been found. If he had he would surely have stayed away but Elliot was now almost beyond rational thought. He was desperate, ill, penniless and homeless and all he could think about was his own survival.

The late autumn chill started to invade his clothing. He needed to know where to go to hitch a lift. Meanwhile he'd look around for somewhere warm to sit for a while. It was beginning to grow dark. The town was busy with teenage pupils hovering around fast food outlets and young mothers, laden with bags, hurrying their youngsters along. He moved into the warmth of a shopping centre and sat down on a seat. Where could he sleep tonight? He looked around. They wouldn't let him stay here, so after a while he went in search of a church in which he could hide and stay the night. He saw one along a side street with a light shining through its open door but just as he got nearer someone closed and locked it. He shuffled along, found a bus shelter and sat down. It was getting colder. He couldn't stay there all night. He'd freeze so he got to his feet and headed out of town to the main road. He needed to get a lift, find a driver who might be going to Gloucester or even Cheltenham.

But luck was not on his side. No-one stopped and, after walking for what seemed miles he flopped, exhausted, in the shelter of some bins at the side of the road. He nibbled a bit of dry bread that he found in his pocket and closed his eyes.

How much later he didn't know but he was woken by something tugging at his coat. As he peered in the moonlight he came face to face with a fox. He struggled to his feet saying, "Shoo -off - b off" and the fox scuttled away leaving Elliot shaking with fear as well as cold.

I can't stay here, he thought and started to walk again, hoping someone would pass by and give him a ride, but nobody wanted to stop in the dark to pick up a strange old man. *All eager to get home to their warm houses I expect*, sighed Elliot with envy.

They say a drowning man sees his life flash before him as he sinks beneath the waves and Elliot, plodding along in the cold, sometimes resting, starving with hunger, hugging his clothes around him, was doing the same. Faces of his loved ones started floating about in his mind, Evelyn, lovely beautiful Evelyn. How he'd adored her. Stephen, his son who he'd used so badly. Celia - ah Celia. I wish we'd had longer together. I'd have been happy forever at Oakdene with you, if you'd lived. Douglas, Sophia --- even Rosina. A fragment of a smile contorted his bearded face as he shuffled along coughing and breathing heavily.

He stumbled on through the night not daring to stop and sleep. Signposts pointing to Gloucester showed that he hadn't gone far. He desperately needed a lift. His experience with the fox had shaken him. As the dawn broke his bones seemed seized up with cold and he was desperately hungry.

He spent the next few days walking and thumbing for lifts. A farmer helped him onto the back of a wagon and carried him a few miles. He pulled up fodder in the fields and gnawed at the raw hardness. He found a few wayside blackberries but slipped into a ditch trying to pick them. He managed to crawl out but found that his ankle hurt and his shoes were full of water. He sat on the grass to empty them and looked for a stick to help him hobble along.

He was a pathetic sight as he wandered through villages picking up a few children's sweets from the ground that they had dropped outside a shop. He was shooed away by a lady waving a broom as he slunk into a garden to steal the peanuts from her bird table. Most people stared at him and hurried away. He didn't realise how terrible he looked. He drank from a dripping rain pipe and sheltered in out buildings and barns when he could. One night he found an unlocked van and stretched out on the seat, sleeping blissfully away from the cold wind.

But the distance he travelled seemed to get no shorter. He had deviated so much that he had missed Gloucester and Cheltenham but when he found himself climbing uphill into the colder air he thought he must be nearly there. *I've reached the Cotswolds. Soon I'll be home,* he thought. Gradually his feet and fingers began to feel numb, his whole body became as if unable to function. His mind and senses were so dulled that he couldn't think properly.

"Bed-- I've found my bed, --- sleep," he muttered as he dropped onto a pile of leaves by the side of the road. He pushed his way in, believing he was covering himself with a duvet. Only his face could be seen as he looked up at the moon rising in the shadowy evening sky.

Had he been more aware he would have realised that he was outside a gateway through which he had passed many times, and embedded in the wall beside this entrance was a sign for the very place that he had been searching, *OAKDENE MANOR.*

He had arrived but did not know it, for this time he closed his eyes and dropped into a sleep from which he would never awaken.

Early the next morning, Gary, the boy who delivered papers, cycled along the road towards Oakdene Manor. The sky was barely light but he could just see the large pile of leaves that had settled to the left of the gateway during the last few days. Like a red rag to a bull he ploughed into it as any boy would in order to make his daily routine more exciting. What he hadn't seen was the solid form of a person lying beneath.

His front wheel, hitting the obstacle, suddenly stopped and Gary pitched over the handlebars and landed in amongst the leaves. His knees grazed the ground ripping a hole in his trousers and he thrust out his hands to save himself as his forehead hit the stone wall.

"Ow-ow-agh," he yelled as pain scorched his knees and hands. He got up gingerly finding that he was basically alright and bent to pick up his bike. It was then that he saw the body that had partially become uncovered, lying still, --- and --- dead.

He stepped back in shock, his eyes opening wide and his mouth gaping like a gulping fish. Then he dropped his bike and ran, down the drive of the Manor and started banging, noisily on the front door.

Anna and James were only just stirring. When Anna heard the knocking she looked at the clock. It was only 7 o clock.

"Whatever ---" she nudged James. "There's someone banging on the door. Listen."

James, grumbling, struggled up out of the warmth of the bed.

The banging by then was becoming frantic so they quickly put on dressing gowns and slippers and hurried downstairs. When they opened the door the poor, frightened shape of the paper boy practically fell inside.

"Gary! Gary! Anna said to the young teenager. "What's up?"

"The--re's a b-b-body --- by the gate, Mrs. S-Shepherd. I f-fell over it."

Anna saw then that blood was oozing through his trousers and his forehead sported a growing lump.

"Come in - come in," she said as she helped the shaking boy inside.

She glanced at James. "I'll go and take a look," he said and reached for his coat and boots.

His heart was pounding as he hurried up the drive and passed through the gateway. He'd seen many dead people due to his work but finding one on his own doorstep was a completely different matter. He saw the pile of leaves that had fallen from the many mature trees that had stood in the grounds for centuries. They had blown into a heap in the corner of the wall.

He moved closer and there it was, a body. He checked for a pulse. There was none. He could see a beard, --- obviously a man, with straggly grey hair - an old man, with features, -- strangely familiar.

"No, no," he gasped, stepping backwards. "It can't be."

He looked again, more closely. There was no doubt. Although the face was older and thinner, it was recognisable. He was definitely looking at ---- .

Turning, James returned down the drive. He didn't hurry as he was concerned about telling Anna. When he walked inside he saw her making some tea for Gary who was sitting in the old chair by the Aga holding an ice pack to his head.

James stood in the doorway, watching, then when she looked up he said,

"Anna, I think you'd better come with me."

The serious expression on his face caused Anna to turn pale. She told Gary to ring home and let them know what had happened to him and where he was, and leaving the boy sipping his tea she followed James outside.

They didn't speak as they walked. Anna kept glancing at James, anxiously , but his face was grim as he took her hand and led her to the pile of leaves.

"Now look carefully, Anna," he said.

She clutched his hand tightly as she peered at the features of the dead man's face. Then she gasped, placing her other hand over her mouth.

"It's him, isn't it? ----- Elliot."

James nodded. "I wasn't sure at first but now that you've recognised him I think that we can be certain that here, lying dead, is the man who stole from us and murdered your father's sister."

They moved some of the leaves to reveal a thin man in tatty clothes and worn out shoes.

"Look at the state of him," said Anna. He's obviously been living rough for ages. It's a long time since Douglas contacted us so he must have been trying to get here all that time."

" --- and he died before he realised that he'd arrived," said James, cynically.

"He left with a fortune and here he is without a penny. Whatever did he do with all our money?" said Anna, sadly.

"We'll probably never know," said James, "but I expect most of it was spent in Hollywood, keeping up with all the glamorous people in the film world."

Anna shivered and took James's arm."Come on, It's cold out here. We'll go back inside and phone the police."

Epilogue

Although Anna and James were both certain that the body was that of Elliot Marshall, the second husband of Anna's mother, the police, when searching through his pockets found passports in the names of Winston Beaumont and Thomas Hughes.

"So he changed his name, frequently," said James. "That figures."

However they were able to check his DNA with a previous sample, and his true identity was confirmed.

When the evidence was conclusive they knew that they must tell Stephen. Anna was quite glad that it was Lucille who answered when she rang. It was obvious to Anna that the news of Elliot's death was a huge relief to her and meant that he could no longer affect their lives. They had obviously been afraid of him turning up, trying to talk himself out of trouble and upsetting them all once more.

They spoke on the phone for a long time, Lucille telling Anna that she would need to choose the right moment to tell Stephen and she hoped that this news would not upset him too much but, instead, stimulate his road to recovery.

They also discussed telling Douglas. Lucille said she'd write to him again. It wouldn't be an easy task. The brothers had been close all their lives until the last few years and however badly Elliot had treated Douglas his death would obviously affect him.

Anna and James arranged a cremation. They were the only mourners. Stephen and Lucille did not attend. The trauma of his father's death had set Stephen back. He had gone very quiet and wouldn't talk even to Lucille which left her very worried about him.

Anna also rang Marcia, who sounded relieved.

"I hesitate to say it, but he got his just deserts, Anna, although I would have liked to see him caught and put on trial for my mother's murder," she said.

Anna covered the funeral expenses in memory of the

few happy years that Elliot had given her mother. His ashes were not buried near Celia, however. Anna and James were not interested in where they were scattered. They did not wish to remember him.

The murder case against him was closed, but the search for their stolen property and money from Oakdene Manor would be ongoing.

A few items and two paintings had turned up but the more time passed the less probable it was that anything else would come to light.

"He only succeeded in destroying himself, James," Anna said as they returned from the funeral. "We still have Oakdene and the estate is doing well. You've only to look at this," she said as she climbed out of the car and walked through the courtyard and saw all the cottages, smartly renovated. They were already starting to get bookings for the next season beginning at Easter. It had been a brilliant idea to convert the old, derelict buildings into holiday homes.

They were now solvent financially and had brought the house and gardens back to their pristine condition. It would all be waiting for Adam when he decided to settle down. He was working, at present, with a charity, in Kenya helping to search for water.

"I'm forever going to be curious, though," said Anna, "as to how he so quickly managed to spend my mother's fortune and dispose of the rest of the paintings."

"We can only imagine," James replied.

Some weeks later they were sitting watching Sky News. During the adverts Anna had gone to the kitchen to make some coffee.

When she returned the News had started again. Suddenly James leant forward and pointed to the screen, "Look, Anna," he said excitedly.

She put down her cup and stared fixedly at the TV. There, smiling, was a face that seemed familiar. The occasion was the premier of a new film, in London, a film that everyone had been talking about, and the leading actress, who was making her debut, stood posing and smiling at the cameras.

"She's beautiful. What's her name?" asked Anna.

"Sophia Ma ----, not quite sure of her second name," said James.

"Have we seen her before, somewhere? Her face looks familiar."

"I think we have," said James. "Remember where we saw Elliot on camera." "In Hollywood, --- of course, ----- escorting this lady."

James had paused the shot and Anna moved closer to study the beautiful film star who filled the screen.

Suddenly she gasped.

"Look at what she's wearing around her neck."

They both saw the glittering diamonds hanging around the slender neck and the three rubies that dangled centrally amongst them.

"I'm certain that's my mother's necklace," said Anna, "given to her by dad on one of their Wedding Anniversaries."

"Are you sure?" asked James. "It would be easy to make a mistake."

"It'll be one of the ones on our list, when we first made it and there'll be a photograph," said Anna, "and if she is the lady that Elliot ran away with, then the necklace will easily be proved as being stolen property."

"Who knows what else he gave her," said James. "Anyway that's another heirloom that we'll hope to get back," he said, giving Anna a hug.

"It'll be a shock to her to have to explain who gave it to her and also to realise that Elliot was nothing but a crook," said Anna.

"I'm sure she'll soon get over it," said James. "There'll be plenty more adoring men who will be eager to replace it."

Anna smiled. "Good luck to her. I hold no grievance against her. She was obviously unaware of what a crook the man was who spent our fortune on her. We've lost a lot but yet survived, James, and we still have the most important part of dad's legacy, Oakdene Manor."

End